BADLANDS BOUNTY

In the badlands at Sweet Spring, Hawkeye Hank and his woman, Meralito, live peacefully. But Horse Soldier — a bounty hunter — arrives in Little Butte, and he's looking for him. He wants to take him back to Texas — dead or alive. Meanwhile, three Texan desperadoes are also on Hank's trail. They shoot Hawkeye's brother-in-law, and along with Horse Soldier, they converge on Sweet Spring. But will Hawkeye Hank escape, or is he fated to be a bounty hunter's reward?

JAMES DEL MARR

BADLANDS BOUNTY

Complete and Unabridged

LINFORD
Leicester

First published in Great Britain in 2010 by
Robert Hale Limited
London

First Linford Edition
published 2012
by arrangement with
Robert Hale Limited
London

British Library CIP Data

Del Marr, James.
    Badlands bounty.- -(Linford western library)
1. Bounty hunters- -Fiction. 2. Criminals- -
Fiction. 3. Western stories.
4. Large type books.
I. Title II. Series
823.9'2–dc23

ISBN 978–1–4448–1022–6

Published by
F. A. Thorpe (Publishing)
Anstey, Leicestershire

Set by Words & Graphics Ltd.
Anstey, Leicestershire
Printed and bound in Great Britain by
T. J. International Ltd., Padstow, Cornwall

This book is printed on acid-free paper

1

Mad Jim Barnaby was sitting right there behind the bar of the Barren Rocks. Everyone called him 'Mad Jim' since he did nothing but mutter to himself all day, sitting back there reading newspapers that were yellow with age. Even his wife Sarah thought he was touched in the head. Only reason she didn't leave him was he kept out of her skirts most of the time. Sometimes she knew he was there only when he cackled with laughter over something he read in those stale pages.

Another thing about Mad Jim was he had Wanted notices pasted up all around the Barren Rocks. Some of them dated back twenty or thirty years, and the faces staring out of them, jaundiced with age, were likely dead even when he stuck them up on the wall.

1

'Why d'you keep those danged creepy posters up on the walls?' one old-timer had asked.

Mad Jim had looked up with a rather startled expression in his loopy brown eyes. 'Company,' he crowed. 'A man needs company around here. Anything wrong with that?'

''T'aint nothing wrong, I guess,' the old-timer said. 'I sometimes think of those days myself. I used to be quick to pull a gun for a shoot out in them days.'

'Echoes of the past,' Mad Jim reflected. 'This here used to be a Pony Express depot when I first moved in. That was a time. I used to keep the horses and run the place. So I decided to stay on. Seemed the best thing to do in the circumstances.'

'No Pony Express now,' the old-timer reflected. 'Was a day I rode real good myself,' he said, with his eyes on the creepy poster back of the bar. 'I could ride them days too. Like the wind, some folks said.'

Mad Jim didn't take him up on that

one. He had had his ration of talk for that day. So he retreated behind the yellowed pages of his newspaper and read on about a famous bank robbery had happened in the year '62, somewhere back in Kansas City.

The old-timer sent a long stream of baccy juice into the spittoon. He knew his cue. So he gathered up his bones and left just as the stranger rode in down what some people might have called Main Street though it was nothing but a sprawl of dust and tumbleweed.

★   ★   ★

The town of Little Butte was hardly a town at all. Just a small cluster of cabins. Not even a bank or a proper saloon. Way back in the old days things had been different. One time it had even supported a hotel that called itself The Way West. Now the hotel building was faded and peeling like most of the other buildings in this almost-ghost

3

town with old men with nothing much to do but smoke their pipes sitting like crows under the ramadas. Young folks did pass by from time to time but they rarely hung around for long. Any stranger would attract immediate attention and send the old folk scurrying about to alert their neighbours.

When this particular stranger rode in he attracted attention of a different sort. The man riding slowly down Main Street seemed in no hurry. Yet he had an aura of purpose about him. You couldn't pin it down but it sent a cold shiver running in your back like somebody had dropped an icicle under your neckerchief. Nobody stirred an inch. Maybe a few curtains twitched but mostly folks just sat staring as though struck dumb as the dust-covered stranger moved through like a ghost.

Sheriff Wills was sitting in his dusty office with the door propped open when the stranger drifted across. The sheriff felt that sliver of ice down his

back like everyone else. As usual he had nothing much to do. There was nobody in the hoosegow, not even the occasional drunken rowdy.

Sheriff Wills was an amiable, slightly overweight man who didn't care for unnecessary exertion. But even he watched the stranger drifting past with some apprehension. He knew his good woman would be looking out too. Maria Wills noticed everything and everyone. She was ambitious. Wanted to set up a business some place to trade in Navajo blankets the Indians brought down from the mountains. But unless things changed, Little Butte wouldn't be any good for that. Maria needed somewhere smart and up-to-date that could welcome travellers from the East.

She peered in though the back door. 'See that man pass?' she asked her husband.

'I saw him,' the sheriff affirmed, 'and I think I know who he is too.'

Maria Wills studied her husband suspiciously. She was a plump, homely

woman who was too bright for a small town like Little Butte. 'Who the hell could a man like that be?' she said. 'Looks like someone just rode in from the smoky regions of Hell.'

'That's the dust,' Sheriff Wills replied laconically.

'Whoever he is he smells like trouble to me.' Maria sniffed and disappeared into the interior from where she could peer out and see where the stranger was headed without looking too much like a busybody.

The smoky regions of Hell. She could be right about that, the sheriff thought to himself, trying to figure out where he had seen the *hombre* before.

★   ★   ★

Now Jude Riverwind was in the Barren Rocks. Nothing unusual about that. Jude was a regular visitor. Never spilled out many greenbacks for drinks but he always sat in his usual place, sometimes talking, sometimes silent as the grave,

which Mad Jim appreciated since he was too busy mumbling to himself and thumbing through those ancient newspapers to bother much.

'What's new?' Mad Jim asked, without looking up from his yellowing page.

Jude raised his eyes under the battered Stetson that looked like all the animals had trampled over it when they rushed out of the Ark, and he cast Mad Jim a look of mild surprise.

'Ain't heard hardly nothing,' he drawled. 'Nothing happens around here. Town's sleepin' like it's waiting for the crack of doom, as you know.'

He ruminated a while, chewing on a plug of tobacco.

''Cept for one thing,' he added, after a minute or two.

'Yeah?' Mad Jim said, from behind his withered page. 'And what would that be?'

Jude chewed on for a while and took a slow sip of his tepid beer. 'About the stranger,' he volunteered, after another long interval.

'What stranger?' Mad Jim murmured without much interest. 'I ain't heard about no stranger.'

Jude had now turned to picking his teeth with a tooth pick. He unwedged a chunk of tobacco and examined it carefully on the spike. Then he flicked it away onto the floor. 'Seen down by the Weedens' spread. Stopped by a day or two back. Seemed to be looking for something or someone. Didn't say what or why. Weeden didn't like the look of him.'

That was a long speech for Jude, the half-breed. Mad Jim laid aside his newspaper with suspicion. 'How come? What did he look like, this stranger?'

Jude reflected deeply. 'Can't say exactly, on account of I didn't see him for myself. Old man Weeden said the *hombre* gave him a creepy feeling like those old-time gun-slingers. Packed a gun and looked like he could use it too.'

'That so?' Mad Jim murmured again.

He was still considering the matter when they heard the sound of a horse

ambling up to the place.

Mad Jim and Jude sat looking at one another in some surprise as the stranger walked right in.

The man was around six feet and he had what one old writer might have called a lean and hungry look. He was well tanned and well muscled like he had been tuning himself up for a good long time. One thing Mad Jim noticed particularly was the hog-leg he had tied down against his thigh. Nothing fancy: just a dark mahogany butt with notches cut into the sides. The holster was dark and well weathered too, leather oiled like it had been kept in good condition just like the man's body, and for some good or evil purpose.

Mad Jim looked the stranger over. 'What can I get you, stranger?' he enquired.

The stranger settled himself down behind a small ramshackle table and nodded. 'Like to bring me a glass of clean water and a whiskey?' he said.

Mad Jim reached up and poured out

a good measure of whiskey.

'Pure spring water, this,' he said, pouring water into a battered mug.

'That so?' the stranger said, with an air of indifference.

'Comes right out of the rocks,' Mad Jim informed him. 'That's why we settled here in Little Butte.'

'You can leave the bottle,' the stranger said, referring to the whiskey.

Mad Jim placed the mug of water and the glass of whiskey and the bottle on the table and went back behind the bar.

★　★　★

'You know what,' Mad Jim said later to Sarah in one of their rare moments of communication, 'when that stranger came into the place I could smell something, and I don't mean sweat or dust or anything like that. It was something more, something like sinister, you know.'

Sarah knew all about her husband's

so-called second sight, but this time she was impressed. She had caught a whiff of sinister herself when the stranger rode up on his pinto. She was feeding the hens and clucking to herself when she saw him tying the horse to the rail. Though the stranger said nothing, a kind of odour came off him and it sure wasn't the odour of sanctity. It was the pungent smell of evil and calculation, she figured. Sarah might have said, 'He moved like a king in his own dark land.' That's the impression he made on her.

★   ★   ★

The stranger nodded and turned to look at the wanted posters pasted on the wall to his left.

'These old Wanted notices?' he enquired, in a deep voice.

'Yes, sir,' Mad Jim said. 'I collect them, keep them for company, kind of.'

'The company of the dead,' the stranger echoed with a humourless grin. 'Most of them in Boot Hill long

past.' He reached out with a long spiky finger and jabbed one of the posters. 'This one is still above the sod, I reckon.' The stranger's finger lingered on the face on the poster and seemed to regard it with a strange relish. 'This one's new,' he said.

'He's new,' Mad Jim agreed. 'That's George James.'

'Ah yes, George James,' the stranger seemed to play with the name. 'Like Jesse and Frank James. George James is an alias for Hawkeye Hank, so I hear.' He paused and studied the poster again. It depicted a somewhat boyish character with a faint line of moustache above his top lip, a man about twenty-nine, maybe thirty, with an expression of faint surprise on his face like he had looked up suddenly and seen a man approaching with a gun.

The stranger turned to Mad Jim and looked at him with eyes as cold as a winter lake. 'You ever hear talk about a Hawkeye Hank around here?'

Mad Jim swallowed with difficulty.

'Only George James like it says on the poster.' His eyes were darting about like he wasn't being strictly honest.

'Could look somewhat different now. Changed his appearance. Might have grown a beard,' the stranger speculated.

Mad Jim looked at Jude Riverwind and tried to swallow, except that something seemed to stick in his windpipe.

The stranger turned to the poster again. 'George James,' he repeated. 'Says here there is a five thousand dollar reward for George James, dead or alive. That's big dollars.'

'Dead or alive, that's right,' Mad Jim agreed. 'Don't know nothing about no alias though.'

The stranger gave Mad Jim a long hypnotic look. 'You happen to know where I can find this *hombre*, Hawkeye Hank?'

Mad Jim had almost retreated behind the long table. He shook his head. 'Couldn't say. I don't know nothing about that. Never seen him, 'cept on

the notice. Like I said, I keep them for company.'

The stranger gave a grim nod. 'It's like this,' he said. 'I've got something for this man Hawkeye Hank, something I'd like to give him.' He showed a row of uneven teeth under his wide brimmed Stetson. 'Could be worth a few dollars, a man could lead me to him.' His searching eyes switched from Mad Jim to Jude Riverwind who was sitting like a stone edifice on the other side of the room.

'Like what few dollars?' Jude River-wind enquired.

The stranger looked him over and nodded. 'That would depend,' he said. 'Are you Apache or Navajo?' he added.

Jude Riverwind didn't care to answer personal questions. His family history had taught him to keep himself to himself. Yet the stranger's riveting eyes seemed to demand an answer. 'What's that to you, stranger?' he asked.

The stranger was still nodding like he had everything worked out in his mind.

'Could be worth something to a man who was half Indian and half gringo,' he said. 'You catch my drift?' He directed his gaze at Jude and Jude had a creepy feeling like the man was burrowing deep into his brain.

'Why half Indian?' he asked.

The stranger was grinning again. 'That's because the Indian part might know something could be interesting.' He topped up his whiskey glass and regarded it sadly as though regretting its passing.

'And what would that be?' Jude asked.

The stranger took a sip of his whiskey. 'This the best whiskey you got?' he asked Mad Jim.

Mad Jim shrugged. 'That's the only whiskey I got.'

The stranger looked down at the liquid and gave it a twirl in his glass. 'You don't get many people passing through,' he said. 'Not like the old-times. This rot gut might be all right for the dead faces on these posters. They

might even enjoy it. A man likes a good stiff whiskey before he takes the long drop, eh?' The stranger gave a low cackle of laughter. He turned his hypnotic eyes on Jude Riverwind again. 'I guess you must be Jude Riverwind,' he said.

Jude's mouth dropped open and he swallowed hard. 'How can you know that?'

The stranger paused. He was in no hurry to speak his piece. After he had taken another swallow of his drink and replenished his glass, he gave Jude a kind of sideways glance. 'Someone told me about you. It doesn't matter who. Gave me quite a good description of you. Said you know every inch of this wilderness.'

Jude was somewhat taken aback, but he clamped his jaw tight to keep from showing it. Old man Weeden never could keep his mouth shut long enough to take a breath.

The stranger was studying the whiskey in the bottom of his glass and

swirling it around like he was reading the runes or seeking the truth in tea leaves. 'Jude Riverwind,' he repeated quietly. 'Pa white gringo, mother Navajo. Born somewhere round Chella Canyon way.' He looked directly at Jude again. 'Would that be right?'

Jude shook his head slightly. This was sort of uncanny.

'You talking to the gringo or the Navajo part?' he asked.

'Depends who wants to listen,' the stranger said.

'What do you want of me?' Jude asked so quietly a mouse might not have heard.

The stranger poured himself another shot and held his glass up to the light. 'The way I figure it,' he said, 'you must know this *hombre* Hawkeye Hank passing well.' He glanced at the face on the Wanted poster briefly. 'Looks harmless enough, doesn't he?'

'Why would that be?' Jude asked.

'That would be because Hawkeye Hank's woman is Navajo. Could even

be some kind of kin to you.'

Jude shook his head. This was more than fortune-telling. Could be some kind of witch doctor stuff. 'I don't have no kin,' he said. 'Specially with Hawkeye Hank and his woman. I ride alone. Have done since I was a raw kid.'

The stranger looked him up and down with steady unrelenting eyes. 'That's good,' he said. 'A man who keeps his own company. That must be rare even out here. 'Cept you talk like you do know Hawkeye Hank.'

He got up from the table and pushed home the cork of the bottle which was now half empty. He went to the bar and placed the bottle under Mad Jim's nose. 'Save this for later. How about if you gave my horse called Jack a piece of fodder and somewhere to bide for the night?'

The old yellow newspaper lay abandoned on the bar. Mad Jim had followed the conversation with some astonishment. He had concluded that

this stranger was some kind of sage or wonder worker, or maybe the Devil himself. 'I guess my woman Sarah can see you right on that,' he said in amazement. 'And what about you? Where will you bide?'

The stranger considered for a moment. 'Called Chiricahua,' he said. 'That's Jack's given name. But I call him Jack. It's shorter and more easy on the tongue. If you happen to have a spare corner somewhere, I'll take it. I'm not particular. Just give me a price and a space, that's all, Just as long as you keep the horse good.'

The stranger went to the door and opened it. He turned and looked back at the two men in the bar.

'Name's Horse Soldier, by the way,' he said. 'That's what they call me, Horse Soldier.'

He closed the door and went out to attend to his horse.

'*Horse Soldier*,' Jude breathed. 'What kind of a name is that?'

Mad Jim was staring at him in

disbelief. 'You never heard of Horse Soldier?'

Jude shook his head slowly. 'I ain't no scholar, Jim. I can't spell out my letters. Never been taught to read.' He paused. 'But now you come to mention it, I do recall the name Horse Soldier somewhat.'

Mad Jim was searching about in his mind, trying to remember what he had read in the newspapers about Horse Soldier and his deeds. 'Don't know why he calls himself Horse Soldier,' he said. 'But I do know one thing: that man who just stepped out of the door is a bounty hunter. That's what he does. He tracks down wanted men and either brings them in or kills them to claim the price on their head. He's kinda professional in that. They say he made a bundle of dollars.'

'You mean he shoots them down dead?' Jude said.

'Didn't I just say that?'

'Just like a rat catcher?' Jude marvelled.

'I read something about him in one of these here newspapers.' Mad Jim fumbled about in a pile of cherished papers behind the table. 'Killed Jeremiah Ridelle some years back. Others, too, just for the reward. Some say they intended to hire him one time to bring in the Kid but Pat Garrett got there first. Horse Soldier is like a wolf. Never lets go. That's what I read. Got it in one of my papers here.' Mad Jim fumbled among the papers on the shelf behind his table but couldn't find the one he was looking for. 'Here somewhere. I can guarantee that,' he muttered to himself.

'Professional and *calculated*,' Jude Riverwind ruminated. 'That don't surprise me. I see it in his eyes soon as he came into the place.'

The two men stared at one another in shocked amazement for several seconds.

'Another thing I remember,' Mad Jim said. 'But that's about Hawkeye Hank.'

Jude looked wary and suspicious. 'What about Hawkeye Hank?' He wasn't going to tell anybody how close he was to Hawkeye Hank and how much reason he had to want to kill him.

'Well' — Mad Jim shook his head — 'I don't like to mention this since you're part Navajo but that price on Hawkeye Hank's head still holds. I asked Sheriff Wills about it last time he drifted in. He says as far as he knows that still has legal application. Told me I should tear the poster down in case it brings me trouble.'

'I guessed that,' Jude said. 'I can't read none but I do have a mite of common savvy. But I don't reckon you'll get much trouble from Hawkeye Hank. He's living real good up there in his hideaway. If George James is Hawkeye Hank he certainly keeps it to himself. That's what I figure anyways.'

'Well, that's good because there's something else you need to know. Maybe you do know already,' Mad Jim said.

'And what would that be?'

'Sheriff Wills says he reckons Hawk-eye Hank has a stash of gold somewhere up there. Could be this Horse Soldier wants to get his hands on it too.'

'That so?' Jude Riverwind marvelled. 'Well, I'll be danged!'

'That is so. On account of they never recovered the gold from that last bank robbery George James pulled off. That's why the price on his head must still hold good.'

'That don't sound too good for Hawkeye Hank,' Jude said. 'That's if he is George James.'

'Specially since this bounty hunter Horse Soldier has his sights on him.'

'That's a fact.' Jude was turning things over in his mind, thinking of the danger to Hawkeye Hank and balanc-ing it against the reward Horse Soldier might be offering to lead him to the place where Hawkeye Hank was holed up. Fact was, Hawkeye Hank wasn't exactly holed up: he was living up in the badland area in a place called Sweet

Spring. Sweet Spring was what it claimed to be, a spring of water gushing out of the rocks in what was otherwise a barren land. Just enough to support a family that wanted to keep out of public notice. A kind of paradise, in fact. Jude Riverwind had been there on occasion but not often since there was bad blood between him and Hawkeye Hank. So he knew exactly where to lead Horse Soldier if he had a mind to it.

'What d'you aim to do?' Mad Jim asked.

Jude was trying to get his mind round the prospects. He was no coward. He had seen men killed before. Often toted a gun himself. He had once fought with a man for three hours before he got the drop on him. But something told him Horse Soldier was in a different category. Horse Soldier had a relentlessness about him, something you could only call dedication. He was like a Jesuit priest with a mission to kill. Horse Soldier was a very dangerous *hombre* indeed!

Jude got up from his seat and pulled on his outer coat. 'What do you suggest I do?' he said tonelessly.

Mad Jim was leaning on the bar. 'Way I see it you got a choice,' he said. 'Either you light out and keep yourself scarce, or you act as guide and lead this Horse Soldier to where he wants to go.' He paused. 'That is if you happen to admit you know where Hawkeye Hank is hanging out which is what I figure.'

Jude didn't say he did and he didn't say he didn't. He stroked his chin thoughtfully and reflected.

'That *hombre* is offering a big reward,' he said. 'I'm wondering what price he has in mind.'

'How much is the life of a man worth?' Mad Jim asked him.

2

Hawkeye Hank was squatting by a fire outside his cabin beside the Sweet Spring. His woman, Meralito, was seated close by, weaving a rug in the traditional Navajo style. When it was finished she would take it to Little Butte probably to Maria Wills who always gave a good deal when she could, or to Hopeful where they had occasional rich visitors from back East. Meralito was an expert weaver in the Navajo way and her work was highly prized. At the moment she preferred to stay right where she was since her belly was swollen with her unborn child, the first she was to bear for Hawkeye Hank.

Hawkeye Hank looked much the same as on the poster, but his pinkish face was partly hidden by a large beard. Since meeting Meralito, apart from the beard, he had adopted the Navajo way

and wore a head band and a golden ear-ring in his right ear. Some might say Hawkeye Hank had gone native, but he didn't see it that way. He had not only adopted the Navajo culture, he felt like a Navajo and, except for the beard and the pink face, he looked like a Navajo. Yes, he was wanted for bank robbery and some said for murder in the name of George James. It was rumoured he had shot down Jeremiah Ridelle to get both shares of the gold they had stolen together way back in Texas. Hawkeye knew there was a price on his head but he didn't think too much about it. He couldn't turn himself in because of Meralito and the unborn child. So he spent most of his time smoking his pipe and looking out across what some might call a barren land — a place he had learned to love. When necessary he went hunting, either alone or with a few Navajo acquaintances, some of them kin to Meralito.

The building behind him was half hogan and half cave. Shaped like a low-squat beehive, it opened out at the back into a network of caves that went deep into the heart of the mountainside. It was a good backdoor through which a man might lose himself or disappear for weeks if necessary. But Hawkeye Hank wasn't thinking about that as he squatted smoking his pipe looking out over the rugged hill with the sound of tumbling spring water singing in his ears.

He saw a figure on horseback weaving its way among the crags and scree. He took out his pipe and watched the rider intently. A familiar figure, that of his brother-in-law, Charlie Silversmith, approached cautiously but confidently. When he came within earshot, Charlie reined in his horse and held up his hand in greeting.

Hawkeye Hank got up from the fire and raised his arm. 'It's Charlie,' he said to Meralito. 'He's come to visit.'

Meralito stopped weaving and turned

to watch the approaching figure. Charlie visited quite often. So they were not surprised.

When Charlie reached them they greeted him without ceremony but with customary Navajo grace. Charlie was married to Nino, Meralito's younger sister.

'Welcome,' Hawkeye Hank said. 'Sit you down by the fire.'

Meralito took Charlie's horse and led it off into the stable where they kept the other horses. A man's horse was his most precious possession among the Indians in these parts.

'What news, Charlie?' Hawkeye Hank asked in Navajo.

'Nothing in particular,' Charlie assured him blandly. Charlie had a large open face like a moon that looked out on the world with pleasure, and the world generally smiled right back at him.

Meralito returned and they spoke about family matters and who was doing this and who was doing that. Then they continued gossiping about

the Navajo and matters relating to the band.

Charlie accepted a pipe of tobacco and smoked with obvious content. Then his brow clouded over and he turned to Hawkeye. 'There is something I should tell you,' he said.

Hawkeye turned to him slowly. He knew Charlie well and could read the occasional clouds that passed over his face. 'What's that?' he asked.

Charlie screwed up his eyes in concentration. 'Did you ever hear tell of a man called Horse Soldier?'

Hawkeye's gaze became suddenly alert and intense. 'Horse Soldier,' he said. 'Yes, I did hear tell of the man. He's a bounty hunter. Why do you ask?'

Charlie waved his pipe in the air and nodded thoughtfully. 'Been seen close by in recent days. Old man Weeden mentioned it when I spoke to him a day or two back. They say he has a mean look about him. Rumour has it he has a reputation as a killer. Been seen in Hopeful and in Little Butte, so they tell

me. Showed up in Mad Jim's place. Heard tell Sheriff Wills is talking about it too. Thought you should know that.'

Hawkeye was stroking his chin. 'Why, thank you, Charlie. I appreciate the warning.'

Nobody mentioned George James or Hawkeye's past. They reckoned that was all behind him since he was now hooked up with Meralito and she was expecting his child. Having a family tends to make a man kind of steady and permanent in his ways.

'Well, I don't know.' Charlie shook his head. 'I just figure you should keep in mind that this mean *hombre* is nosing around down there somewhere. Can't be for nothing, can it?'

After supper, it was still daylight, so Charlie decided to pull out and ride back in the direction of the Reservation. Hawkeye Hank and Meralito sat looking at one another across the fire. Though Meralito had her own mind about things, she waited for her man to

speak first. Hawkeye Hank had disappeared into the hogan and come out with his Winchester '73. Meralito watched as he oiled it and cleaned it up.

'You know what?' Hawkeye Hank said.

'What?' Meralito was no great talker despite the fact she knew her own mind.

Hawkeye Hank was rubbing the mechanism down with a piece of oily rag. Apart from his woman and his horse, that Winchester was the most precious thing in his life.

'What I think is,' he said, 'you should go back to your kin for a while and stay with them till the baby is born.'

Meralito looked at him blankly and remained as still as the rocks around them.

Hawkeye Hank tossed his head. 'Sure,' he said. 'But we got to think about the baby, don't we?'

Meralito kept looking at him for a while in that deep unfathomable way. 'I'm staying,' she said. 'This is my home and I'm staying.'

Meralito knew something about Hawkeye's past but not everything. She didn't know whether he had killed men or not, or how many, but she did know there was a price on his head. That meant that some day someone would come looking for him and that someone could be the man called Horse Soldier.

★　★　★

Come morning, Horse Soldier was sitting in the bar of Barren Rocks taking his chow. He had spent the night on a hard, creaking mattress up in the loft. It was by no means luxurious, but he had slept well, and the breakfast Sarah had provided, though nothing special, was lavish and filling: ham and eggs and beans. Mad Jim wasn't reading his yellowing newspapers, he was out there in the yard splitting logs. Sarah fussed about, cleaning spilt booze off the bar; there was nobody else around. Horse Soldier had a mug of coffee on the table in front of him and what was left of the

bottle of whiskey beside it. He poured an ample measure into his coffee and onto his ham and beans, taking care to avoid flooding his over-and-easy eggs.

This *hombre* sure cares a lot for his booze, Sarah Barnaby thought, as she wiped away the beer stains on the bar.

'Aiming to stay long?' she asked him.

Horse Soldier paused in his eating and gave her a long and level look with his penetrating eyes. 'Who wants to know?' he asked.

Sarah shook her head. 'That's no never mind to me,' she said. 'I was thinking about the horse, Jack.'

Horse Soldier nodded and seemed satisfied. 'Jack treats me good,' he said. 'Always take care of a good piece of horse flesh. Comes back at you in the end.'

'That's what Jude Riverwind says,' Sarah agreed. 'Treat a horse good and he always treats you the same, that's what he says.'

Horse Soldier looked up again with his keen penetrating eyes. 'You know

where Jude Riverwind bides?' he asked.

Sarah shook her head. 'I don't rightly know about that. Nobody knows much about Jude Riverwind. He sort of drifts in and out. He has that Indian way with him, a kind of rootlessness. Might drop in later, and might not. You never can tell with Jude.'

'Doesn't spend a deal of dollars, I notice,' Horse Soldier observed.

'Just comes in for company,' Sarah said. 'You haven't got it, you can't spend it. That's a fact can't be denied.'

Horse Soldier nodded again. 'Just so long as you look after Jack, I'll pay you good.'

Sarah didn't know what to make of that. Seemed like Horse Soldier couldn't give a straight answer to anything except about the horse.

* * *

Sarah went out into the yard and Mad Jim gave her a sideways glance and took a breath from his log splitting.

'Like his breakfast good, did he?' he asked.

Sarah stood with her knuckles pressed against her amble hips. 'I don't like that man,' she said. 'Gives me a right creepy feeling.'

Mad Jim laid his axe aside and mopped his brow with a rag. 'Pays good dollars, don't he?'

'It ain't that,' she said. 'It's the way he looks at folk with those searching eyes of his. Seems to stare right into a body's soul like the Archangel Gabriel or something.'

Mad Jim had no answer to that. He had observed the same himself, but he rarely agreed with his wife on principle.

'I think you should get back in there,' she said. 'Could be drinking up all your booze while you're out here. That's another thing I learned. That man's got a great thirst for whiskey.'

Mad Jim couldn't disagree with that either, but he took the point and went back inside.

Horse Soldier was still sitting at the table. But there was a difference. He had finished his breakfast and he had a Colt revolver in his hand.

Mad Jim froze in the doorway as Horse Soldier turned towards him. Horse Soldier was shaking with silent laughter, but there was no humour in his laugh. He raised his shooter, examined it carefully, and laid it on the table beside him.

'Know where I can locate Jude Riverwind?' he asked. 'Need to talk to him again. About money, you know what I mean?'

Jim shook his head and moved behind the bar where he reached for a glass to polish. 'Never know with Jude,' he said. 'Could be he lit out for somewhere. Gone hunting, maybe. Don't stay long in one place. That's Jude. Could be gone ten days, a month, maybe. Impossible to say.'

'Does he have a wife, a woman of

some kind?' Horse Soldier asked.

Mad Jim shook his head. 'That I wouldn't know. Jude never talks about those things. Likes to keep hisself to hisself.'

As Mad Jim watched, Horse Soldier held the Colt low and started loading it with slugs. Looked like a .45. He was still holding the Colt when they heard the noise of an approaching horse. A bit early in the day for visitors, Mad Jim thought, but then a shadow fell across the doorway and a man of middle years came in. He was about 5' 10" or 11" and had a fairly substantial paunch, over which he wore a striped vest. Over the vest he wore a long jacket that came to just above his knees. On his head was a dark fedora-like hat. Standing in the doorway with his thumb hooked into his belt, he gave a glimpse of a gun holster. Despite his paunch you had the immediate impression that he could draw as fast as a snake if he wanted to. He seemed to take a quick

note of the gun in Horse Soldier's hand and dismiss it.

Horse Soldier, Mad Jim noticed, had tensed up as the man appeared in the doorway, but now he relaxed again. He slid the Colt back into its holster.

The visitor came into the room and rested his elbows on the bar. 'Just thought I'd drop in for a visit,' he said. He had a surprisingly light tenor voice. Sounded as though he wouldn't harm a fly.

'Why sure, Sheriff,' Mad Jim said in a sort of fluster. 'Always glad to see a man of the law. What can I get you?'

'Just give me a beer,' the sheriff said. He turned to Horse Soldier. 'You just rode in yesterday,' he said.

'You're an observant man of the law,' Horse Soldier agreed.

The sheriff eyed him with twinkling suspicion. 'You wouldn't be Horse Soldier, would you?'

'I might be,' Horse Soldier said. 'Depends who wants to know?'

'Sheriff Wills wants to know,' the

sheriff said. 'I knew I'd seen you somewhere before.'

'Where would that be?' Horse Soldier said.

The sheriff nodded. 'Seen a picture of you somewhere. Standing side by side with Pat Garrett, as I remember. May I enquire what brings you to these parts?'

Horse Soldier gave a faint, contemptuous shrug. 'Just passing along through,' he said. 'Could be I'm doing research on the old days. Heard tell they had some interesting things happening in these parts back then. Pony Express station, so I heard.'

Sheriff Wills closed one eye and squinted at the stranger. He knew humour when he saw it, but this man had a sombreness about him that chilled your bones. 'That name Horse Soldier, that your real born name?'

Horse Soldier cocked one eye. 'Could be, my ma never told me that. My pa was a soldier, so she said. Indian fighter. So she called me Soldier. Never

knew him and he never knew me. So I can't be sure.'

Wills nodded. Another joke to add to his collection.

'Horse,' the stranger added. 'I just like horses better than people. So my ma called me Horse. That's what they tell me. What's in a name, anyway?'

Wills blew the froth off his beer and sipped it thoughtfully. 'Could be a lot in a name,' he reflected. 'Some say a man is shaped by his name.'

Horse Soldier stared straight back at him and nodded. 'I wouldn't know too much about that. I just know about horses and my job.'

Wills took a long swig. Then wiped his mouth with the back of his hand. He had a grizzled beard stained around the mouth with nicotine.

'That brings me to another question,' he said. 'What exactly is your job?'

Horse Soldier raised an eyebrow. 'Debt collector, you could say. I mostly please myself, but from time to time, I collect debts.'

'Heard about you,' the sheriff said casually.

Horse Soldier grinned. 'Not only the picture of me and Pat Garrett, I guess.'

Wills grinned right back at him. 'You say debt collector. I read in the papers a while back you're a bounty hunter. You go for men with a price on their head. Is that right?'

'Could be,' Horse Soldier replied without commitment. 'Depends what's around. What else did you hear?'

Wills gnawed his beard with his two front teeth. 'Heard tell you never give up until you got your reward. They say you made yourself passing rich with that Colt revolver of yours.'

'That's what they say,' Horse Soldier agreed. 'That's part of the code.'

'A man can get himself big dollars that way,' Wills speculated.

Horse Soldier moved his head from side to side. 'Maybe you should try it yourself sometime. You could end up rich if you make the right investments.'

Mad Jim had listened to this

conversation with growing anxiety. Now he flinched slightly as Sheriff Wills swung slowly to him. Jim had picked up one of his papers, pretending to read. He held the yellowed paper against his chest and looked at the sheriff apprehensively. He didn't care too much for the turn the conversation had taken.

'That there poster you got pasted to your wall,' the sheriff said. 'That's recent, ain't it?'

'Haven't had it long,' Mad Jim agreed. 'I keep them for company as you know, Sheriff.'

'Heard tell you talk to them from time to time,' Wills speculated.

Mad Jim looked blank. 'That's just fanciful,' he said.

'Did they ever answer back?' the sheriff asked.

'Not so I heard,' Mad Jim replied with a faint smile.

Wills swung towards the poster close by where Horse Soldier was sitting. 'That one there,' he said. 'George James. Kind of purty face like the Kid.

Most of the others are dead and gone, but he's recent. I've got another picture in my office. There's still a reward on his head. I believe it says five thousand dollars, dead or alive?'

'That is so,' Mad Jim said. 'That's what it says.'

The sheriff glanced in Horse Soldier's direction again. 'Could be that's why you're here, to claim that reward,' he suggested. 'Is that possible?'

Horse Soldier nodded. 'Could be,' he agreed. 'Depends on whether George James is a man called Hawkeye Hank.'

Sheriff Wills cleared his throat and intervened. 'Well, I guess I should warn you, Mr Horse Soldier. If you're looking for Hawkeye Hank, that's a wild country up there. A man could get lost for days. You go up here it could be your last ride.'

'Is that your opinion, Sheriff?' Horse Soldier said.

'That is my opinion,' the sheriff replied.

Horse Soldier chewed over the

matter. 'A man rides until he falls,' he said. 'All through history that's been happening. But that doesn't stop a man from riding, does it?'

* * *

Hawkeye Hank was not easily put out. In the old days he would have been fatalistic about what the future held for him. Either he lived or died. That was the way things were. But now the cards were stacked differently. He had a family to consider and that made him responsible . . . responsible but restless. He figured he owed everything to Meralito and that unborn child. He was still pondering on what he should do when he saw another rider approaching the place. It wasn't Charlie this time, but it was someone else he recognized, someone who recalled a past he didn't want to think about too much.

He was standing still as a stone among the rocks close to the Sweet Spring with the Winchester cradled in his arm.

45

The man stopped at a distance and raised his arm. 'I come in peace, brother,' he called out.

Hawkeye Hank moved his head slightly but didn't reply. He kept his hand on the Winchester.

'Got something to discuss with you,' the other man said.

'Say your piece from where you are, and git,' Hawkeye Hank said, bringing the Winchester round to cover the intruder. He could see the man had a gunbelt strapped to his thigh.

The man shrugged and made no move. 'You want to parley with me from here?' he asked laconically.

'I don't want to parley with you from anywhere,' Hawkeye Hank replied.

The man sat his horse with an air of nonchalance. 'Could be to your advantage,' he said. 'Like a lot of driftwood has passed on down the river since those bad times.'

'If you've come to tell me there's a man called Horse Soldier nosing around, forget it,' Hawkeye Hank said.

'I heard it already.'

Jude Riverwind gave a faint nod. 'Horse Soldier is around,' he agreed. 'I seed him in the Barren Rocks place. We spoke together. I hear he's staying around for some reason.'

'So what reason would that be?'

'That might mean he thinks you bear a marked resemblance to a man called George James, wanted for murder, dead or alive. Leastways, that's what it says on the poster. Dead or alive, it says. I seen it in Mad Jim's place.'

Hawkeye Hank was none too impressed by that. 'Is that all you've got to tell me?'

Jude sidled up closer and stopped when he saw Hawkeye Hank's Winchester move to cover him. 'This Horse Soldier offered me a deal, I could lead him up here to your place.'

'What was the deal?'

Jude Riverwind cocked his head on one side. 'I come clean with you, Hawkeye. He offered me maybe a thousand dollars,' he lied.

'A thousand dollars!' Hawkeye Hank laughed. 'You mean he offered you a thousand dollars for my scalp?'

Meralito suddenly appeared from the hogan, standing a little to the right of her man. She had a small chopping-axe in her hand.

'A thousand there about,' Jude Riverwind lied again. 'We didn't do no deal. I don't do deals like that.'

'Then what's on your mind?' Hawkeye Hank asked him. He glanced beyond Jude Riverwind towards the rocks. Maybe Horse Soldier was up there somewhere drawing a bead on him. That way, Jude Riverwind would earn his one thousand dollars.

Jude Riverwind shrugged. 'Thought you and me could do a deal,' he said. 'You and me. I lead this Horse Soldier up somewhere else. You kill him. That way he don't bother you no more.'

'And you don't get the thousand dollars either. I don't catch your drift.'

Jude Riverwind urged his mount forward a little more. 'Things have been

bad between us, Hawkeye. Could be I want to put things right. Maybe the dollars don't matter none to me.'

Hawkeye studied the man thoughtfully. Could it be true Jude Riverwind didn't care about the dollars? Hawkeye's mind went back a few years to the time he met Meralito when he was hiding out up here in the so-called badlands. He had a bullet lodged in his shoulder from a gunfight he'd been in and it could have gone gangrenous. Meralito and Charlie had drawn that slug out of his shoulder and bound it up. Meralito had nursed him back to health, and that was when it had started.

The trouble was, at that time Jude Riverwind wanted Meralito for himself and thought he had her. So there had always been bad blood between Hawkeye Hank and Jude Riverwind. At one time Riverwind had even taken a gun to Hawkeye and would have shot him dead if Charlie hadn't intervened. Charlie had clubbed Riverwind down

and knocked him out. Hawkeye could have shot him but he held back. A man doesn't forget a thing like that.

Hawkeye was about to speak, but Meralito suddenly moved forward with her chopping axe. 'Listen, Jude,' she said, 'and hear what I say.' She took a step forward, staring straight, into Riverwind's eyes. 'I don't know what is in your heart but you'd better think again.'

It was a short speech, but it was enough. Jude Riverwind drew back and averted his eyes. 'OK, I'll back off.' He took the reins of his horse and turned. Then he paused and looked over his shoulder. 'But don't say I didn't warn you, Hawkeye. Don't say I didn't warn you. This man Horse Soldier wants to kill you and he's plenty mean. He has a lot of scalps on his belt and he's a killer. So don't say I didn't warn you.'

He ambled down the trail that led away from Sweet Spring, and rode steadily on without looking back once.

Hawkeye Hank and Meralito watched

him until he was no more than a cloud of rising dust. Then Hawkeye Hank turned to Meralito and he saw a look of concentration he had seen only once before and that was when she first saw the wound on his shoulder.

'You know something,' he said, 'that man has a tongue like a rattlesnake. Can't tell which way his brain is working.'

'I think he wants to kill you,' Meralito said.

3

Hopeful was a small town slightly east of Little Butte. To Eastern eyes it might have been a ghost town because like Little Butte there wasn't much to it, but some folk said that was part of its charm. Its hotel and main saloon was called the Old Bison Saloon.

Right now three men were sitting at a table in the saloon engaged in a game of poker. The owner of the saloon, Jack Logan, didn't care for the look of them but business was business and you couldn't turn away good money.

One of the men was Laramie Pete. He had a deep brown visage, cracked all over like leather that was splitting apart. The second man was younger and smoother. He was called Handsome Johnny. That was what some of his lady friends called him on account of his regular good looks.

The third man had a permanent grin on his face like there was always something to laugh about. He had a spasmodic twitch around his right eye, though nobody cared to mention it in case he turned even uglier. His name was Tod Ridelle and he was the kid brother of Jeremiah Ridelle, the man George James, alias Hawkeye Hank, had shot to death some years back. That killing had become a family legend like a throbbing abscess that refuses to heal, and Tod Ridelle had grown up with the notion that one day he would avenge his brother's death and reclaim the stash of gold Jeremiah and George James had stolen. Now, it seemed, he had his chance.

Restless Handsome Johnny was studying his hand of cards with angry eyes. He was a man who could never keep still for longer than a second and he had little patience for card games or anything that stood in his light. Now he threw his cards on the table and said, 'I'm out!' He hauled himself to his feet.

'I'm getting sick of poker, anyway! And I'm tired of sitting around here like we're waiting for Christmas to come!'

He walked away from the table and squinted out of the window. All he saw was other buildings looming like phantoms in a fog of dust and tumbleweed. Hopeful was not the kind of town a man who liked the bright lights could appreciate. Not the kind of place you would want to stay unless you were hiding from the law.

'Thought you promised action?' he said to Tod. 'I don't see any action. Where's the action you promised? Where's the pot of gold at the end of the rainbow?'

'You wanna cash in your chips?' Laramie Pete said, stretching out a horny hand to inspect Handsome Johnny's discarded cards.

'I always get a dead hand,' Handsome Johnny complained. 'They call it Fate or something, but maybe it's the way you deal them out.'

Laramie looked at him poker-faced.

You couldn't guess he was the kind to draw on a man who cheated and shoot him under the table. 'You aim to put in a complaint?' he said in a voice as deep and cracked as the lines on his face.

Handsome Johnny stamped around a bit. 'I can't sit around rotting like this any longer. I need some kind of action.'

He strutted up and down beside the window, peering out this way and that and seeing nothing but the dust storm outside. The others knew that when Handsome Johnny was in that mood he might just go out and bust up the town — what there was of it, which wasn't much to crow about anyway.

Tod Ridelle's right eye had started to twitch and he was grinning like a cat with a twist in its tail. 'Don't get yourself in a sweat, man,' he said. 'I reckon we be ready to move out come morning. Yellow Tail drifted in last night.'

'Yellow Tail!' Handsome Johnny jeered. 'That some sort of bird, or calico queen, or something?' Everyone knew Yellow

Tail was an Indian guide who hung around waiting for someone to give him a dollar or two and a bottle of hooch.

Laramie Pete gave a dry laugh. 'You don't say,' he said. You could see his larynx wobble from side to side when he spoke.

'Talked to him earlier.' Tod Ridelle said.

Handsome Johnny came back and placed his hands on the table and leaned forward to peer into Tod Ridelle's eyes. 'What did this Yellow Tail Indian say then?'

Ridelle's right eye was twitching even more than usual. 'Yellow Tail says he knows where George James who calls himself Hawkeye Hank is holed up. Place called Sweet Spring, close to the Navajo Reservation. Says we could take him easily. Hawkeye Hank has gone soft like a jelly ever since he jumped the lariat with that Navajo woman of his. Sits up there smoking and guarding his pot of gold all day like he don't know what to do with it. We could ride in, take him, claim the

reward, pick up the pot of gold, which is mine by rights anyway, and set ourselves up in the world.'

Handsome Johnny drew back thoughtfully and sat down again. 'That's the pot of gold you say Hawkeye Hank stole from your brother.'

'That's the way it was.' Tod Ridelle was grinning but he didn't look pleased. 'That gold is rightfully mine, I tell you.'

'Sounds good,' Laramie Pete ruminated, 'but we help you to find it, what's in it for us? You got to make that clear.'

Tod Ridelle nodded. 'You get your cut of the five thousand,' he said, 'and, if we lay our hands on that gold, I'll cut you in on that too. That's the deal.'

Laramie Pete and Handsome Johnny exchanged glances. Handsome Johnny nodded. 'So that's what we do?' he said. 'We ride in, do the business, and then out again just like a bunch of monkeys escaped from a zoo.'

Tod Ridelle's face twitched nervously. 'I want that gold because by rights it's mine. My brother Jeremiah would want it for me. And I want Hawkeye Hank's blood. Blood for blood, that's what it says in the Good Book. Matter of honour. That's what I mainly want. I want that squaw man dead.'

Laramie Pete nodded solemnly. 'That's OK,' he announced, ''cept for one thing.'

'What's that thing? Tod Ridelle asked.

Laramie Pete raised his eyes and looked round the table gravely. 'I heard a rumour, that's all.'

'What rumour was that?' Handsome Johnny asked. He knew Laramie Pete had connections, some of them in the air, or so it seemed.

'You ever hear tell of the man called Horse Soldier?' Laramie Pete gave them a look of stern enquiry.

Nobody replied for a moment. Then Handsome Johnny piped up. 'You talking about Horse Soldier they call a

bounty hunter?'

'He doesn't call himself a bounty hunter, he *is* a bounty hunter,' Laramie Pete replied.

'What's with this Horse Soldier?' Tod Ridelle asked contemptuously.

'Just that someone said Horse Soldier is in the county right now. Nobody knows why. Could be he's looking for Hawkeye Hank like us. Wants to claim the reward, maybe find the gold too.' There was a momentary pause. Laramie Pete was thoughtfully gnawing his lip.

'That what you heard?' Tod Ridelle said.

'That's the truth,' the bartender piped up from behind the bar.

Three pairs of eyes swivelled towards him. That bald headed bartender was none too bright. He had heard the whole conversation and he figured he could ingratiate himself with these wild-looking men, maybe earn a few extra bucks too.

'Where d'you hear that?' Handsome Johnny barked out.

'Common knowledge,' the bartender said. 'Everyone knows everything that happens around here. Matter of interest, old man Weeden told me when he came in the other night.'

'You know about a place called Sweet Spring?' Handsome Johnny asked him.

The bartender shrugged. 'Heard about it. Never been there myself. That's real wild country up there. A man could easily get lost, so they tell me.'

Handsome Johnny was prowling around. The notion of wild country didn't worry him. He might like the bright lights and the calico queens, but he also liked a challenge and riding up into the wild country to shoot down a renegade appealed to his sense of adventure. Bringing down Horse Soldier was another challenge but that gave spice to the first.

'Sooner we hit the saddle the better,' he said. 'While we're sitting around here, playing poker and drinking bad whiskey, that Horse Soldier could be

getting a bead on Hawkeye Hank ready to shoot him down.'

'Don't know much about Horse Soldier,' Tod Ridelle said. 'Could be he's just passing through.'

Laramie Pete grinned. 'Horse Soldier doesn't just pass through. He comes with purpose. He's dedicated. It's what he does. You could call him a professional in that. Ruthless too. I should know: I rode with him once.'

The other two turned to look at Laramie Pete in some surprise.

'You mean you rode with Horse Soldier?' Handsome Johnny was grinning with incredulity.

'Sure I rode with him. Brought one or two in with him, claimed a few rewards with him one time. I know the way he works and he's pretty deadly. Never misses a trick and never wastes a bullet.'

Handsome Johnny chuckled. 'You know him well enough to read his thoughts?'

'Nobody reads Horse Soldier's thoughts,'

Laramie Pete replied. 'You ride with him a million years, you wouldn't guess what he's thinking. Tell you one thing, though, Horse Soldier has a kind of code. He's cold as a snake and he always knows what he's doing. Goes right for the jugular when he strikes. We have to bear that in mind.'

There was a moment's silence.

'Then maybe we have to kill him too,' Tod Ridelle speculated.

'That could be so,' Laramie Pete agreed. 'I guess I owe him that too.'

'How come?' Handsome Johnny asked.

'A bullet from a Winchester grazed my head. Still have headaches to prove it. Horse Soldier happened to be at the trigger end at the time.'

Handsome Johnny grinned. 'That gives you something to get even with on Horse Soldier,' he said.

Laramie Pete chewed his lip. He didn't reply.

★   ★   ★

Horse Soldier was still around the Barren Rocks. Mostly he sat out on the back porch smoking an Indian pipe. It looked like a pipe of peace with its beaded stem but, as the smoke curled up into the quiet reflective air it spoke more of a relentless purpose than of peace. Horse Soldier was waiting, waiting patiently as though he knew what was coming but wasn't sure when it would arrive.

He watched Sarah throwing out feed for the hens, hanging wet clothes from a line rigged from a post at the corner of the cabin. And still he waited, smoking his pipe and scanning the rugged mountains beyond. Those mountains changed colour, he noticed. Sometimes they looked apricot colour with the sun on them. Other times they were grey and sombre like menacing cats crouching ready to pounce.

Horse Soldier watched and waited. The meals were passing good and Jack, his horse, seemed content grazing in the paddock. But dollars don't last for

ever and Horse Soldier knew sooner or later he had to make a move.

He was still waiting and watching when he saw a horseman approaching slowly amidst a cloud of dust. Horse Soldier grinned thinly to himself. He knew that the wind was shifting and his patience was about to be rewarded.

The rider rode right up to the spread. He took his mount into the paddock and let it drink. Then he came closer and raised his hand.

'Guess you're still around,' he said. It was Jude Riverwind.

'Waiting,' Horse Soldier replied laconically. He shifted his Stetson away from his eyes and watched as the half breed came closer to the cabin. Horse Soldier saw he was tooled up with a Remington at his side.

Sarah bustled away with her basket and disappeared from view.

'You still want to do business?' Jude Riverwind said.

Horse Soldier looked at him straight. 'What kind of business?'

Jude Riverwind returned his look and held it, but only for a second before his gaze went off to the left. 'Business like you said last time we met.'

The thin smile returned to Horse Soldier's face. 'You want to do some kind of a deal?'

Jude Riverwind was perplexed and uneasy. How do you do a deal with a *hombre* who gives you a question for a question? 'Said you were looking for Hawkeye Hank. Had something for him. That's what I remember.'

Horse Soldier gave a slight, almost imperceptible nod. 'Could be,' he said nonchalantly. 'So what?'

'Said there could be something for me too, I take you to him.'

Horse Soldier tipped his hat again. 'You have something in mind?' he asked.

Jude Riverwind held his head on one side. Sure, he had something in mind. He had quite a lot in mind. 'Could be a thousand dollars,' he suggested.

Horse Soldier considered the matter.

Then he looked up. 'I didn't hear you right. I thought you said a thousand dollars.'

'That's what I said,' Jude Riverwind repeated. 'One thousand dollars. I take you there. You give Hawkeye Hank what you come to give him. That's the deal.'

Horse Soldier sucked on his Indian pipe for thirty seconds. Like in poker, a man doesn't show his hand unless he's ace high. 'Tell you what I'll do,' he said at length. 'I'll give you five hundred flat.'

Jude Riverwind looked thoughtful and then shook his head. 'Five hundred's not enough. Hawkeye Hank maybe not like what you bring. You know Hawkeye is not Hawkeye for nothing. He looks and sees. He's a straight shooter too. You give me one thousand and it's a deal.'

Horse Soldier was still grinning behind the cloud of smoke that rose from his pipe. 'Five hundred is enough for acting postman. I'll give you five

hundred and, if we bring him in, there's another five hundred for you. That means you get a clear thousand when the job is finished.'

Jude Riverwind nodded but still he wasn't satisfied. 'I don't bring him in. I lead you to him: you bring him in.'

Horse Soldier took his pipe out of his mouth and inspected it. 'When will you be ready to move?'

'We move at sunup tomorrow,' he said.

They didn't shake hands. A man should have trust before he shakes hands on a deal.

★   ★   ★

Charlie Silversmith, Hawkeye's brother-in-law, liked to go hunting alone. He liked the old ways. He had a vivid memory of the time when he did his vision quest when he was no more than fifteen summers old. He had climbed up into the chosen place among the rocks and sat there fasting for three days and nights before the eagle spirit

came and spoke to him.

The eagle descended and unfurled its great wings. Charlie couldn't see its face because the sun was behind the bird. But he could make out its curved beak as it turned its head towards him. And then it spoke.

'You have been patient,' it said in a strange birdlike tone. 'And now I come in answer to your quest to give you your secret name.'

The bird lowered its great head and spoke Charlie's hidden name, the name he would keep in his heart for ever.

The bird also told Charlie that he had secret powers. He would read men's minds and heal their hearts. But he must also be as strong and as brave as an eagle.

Charlie always carried that vision in him wherever he went. That was why he liked riding alone among the mountains that were his home. Sometimes he rode alone. At other times he rode with a kinsman and, occasionally, with Hawk-eye Hank, his brother by blood. Though

Hawkeye Hank was a white gringo, he had become a blood brother and Charlie had a powerful bond with him.

Charlie was riding in the hills one day close to Hopeful when he saw Yellow Tail far away down below. Charlie had no liking for Hopeful or Little Butte. He thought of it as a town of cold, pale men and the ghosts of the dead. When he looked down on the town he saw many phantoms drifting along the streets like tumbleweed.

He had little regard for Yellow Tail either. Yellow Tail was part Apache. But he had gone bad according to Charlie's calculations. Yellow Tail would do almost anything for a bottle of white man's booze and sometimes he would lie for days in a drunken stupor anywhere he fell. But Yellow Tail was not a fool. In the past he had been an expert tracker and a useful man to hunt with. So he might be a man to be wary of, particularly when he rode into a town like Hopeful.

Seeing Yellow Tail needed investigation. So Charlie rode down slowly getting close to the outer buildings of the town. He saw Yellow Tail close in on the Old Bison Saloon. This might be worth investigating specially since Charlie had heard rumours about three strangers staying in the place. That and what Charlie had discovered about Horse Soldier gave him some cause for concern.

Charlie tethered his mustang in a patch of mesquite close behind the place and mooched in low where he might get a fix on Yellow Tail. The Old Bison, Charlie thought. He remembered the days when the bison roamed the plains. That was before the buffalo hunters came to ravage the place and drive the beasts almost to extinction.

He watched Yellow Tail dismounting. Now he seemed to be waiting under the ramada. His body movements suggested he was reluctant to go in through the doorway. Charlie knew how he felt. Yellow Tail might be a drunk but he still

had a sense of self-preservation.

As Charlie raised his big moon face for a better look at Yellow Tail, a man came out to join Yellow Tail under the ramada. It was Tod Ridelle though Charlie didn't know that. Yellow Tail and Tod Ridelle were talking now, gesturing with their hands and making some kind of bargain. He slid closer to listen. Because of the gusty wind he caught only snatches of what they were saying.

★ ★ ★

Tod Ridelle stood under the sign of the Old Bison staring at Yellow Tail. Yellow Tail looked like a lizard that had crawled in out of the sun. His buckskin jacket and his leg garments were stained and creased and brown as though he had spent most of his life sleeping under a dusty rock. His face was lined and creased like Laramie Pete's, only worse. He had the crazed look of the living dead in his eyes. Not a

man you could like or trust.

'I'm ready,' he said through his carious teeth. 'I take you to that place, show you where Hawkeye Hank and his woman live. They call it Sweet Spring.' When he brought out the word *sweet* the reek of his whiskey breath came at Tod Ridelle like the stink from one of the seven circles from Hell.

'We go there at sunup tomorrow,' Tod Ridelle said.

'You give me good whiskey?' Yellow Tail said. It was more a demand than a question.

'Sure I give you whiskey,' Tod agreed. 'I give you plenty whiskey.'

'Give me whiskey right now,' Yellow Tail demanded.

Tod Ridelle swayed in the doorway. 'I give you whiskey, you won't be fit to lead us to Sweet Spring,' he said. 'You'll be laid out dead drunk under the sidewalk here.'

Yellow Tail shook his shaggy head. 'I don't drink too much. You follow me, I take you there.' He took a gasping

breath. 'I will show a good place so you can gun down on Hawkeye Hank. It is safe, a ledge where you look down and shoot. It will be easy. Like shooting antelope.' This was a surprisingly long speech for Yellow Tail.

'OK,' Tod Ridelle said. 'I'll give you a small bottle now. After you lead us to Hawkeye Hank you can have as much as you can drink for the rest of your life.'

Yellow Tail showed the decaying remains of broken teeth.

'I come at sunup,' he said.

Yellow Tail turned and vanished like another ghost in that dusty town.

Tod Ridelle turned and saw Handsome Johnny standing behind him.

'So that's your famous tracker!' Handsome Johnny jeered. 'Never trust an Indian who drinks.'

Tod Ridelle stuck his twitching face forward belligerently. 'You got a better idea?'

Handsome Johnny shrugged and went back into the saloon.

Charlie Silversmith watched from cover as Yellow Tail drifted away like the tumbleweed. He hadn't heard everything but he had heard enough. He moved like a shadow between the tumbledown buildings of the town and made for the stand of mesquite where he had left his horse.

As he approached, he saw the horse and something else. A man was standing close by and he had a gun in his hand. The gun was pointing at Charlie and the man was Laramie Pete.

'Hello, Injun,' Laramie Pete said. 'Did I interrupt you in something?'

* * *

Charlie Silversmith wasn't the only one who had heard Tod Ridelle and Yellow Tail talking under the ramada. Jack Logan, the owner of the Old Bison, was also hovering close. Jack Logan had been around Hopeful for more years

than he could remember. He knew most everyone in the territory. He was a friend of old man Weeden and Mad Jim and was familiar with all the gossip. So he already knew about Horse Soldier, the bounty hunter. He also knew about the squaw man Hawkeye Hank living up at Sweet Spring, though he had never met him. Sheriff Wills was a friend and an occasional drinking partner. Sometimes the sheriff came down to Hopeful to exchange news with Sheriff Ames, the sheriff of Hopeful. The two would sit in the Old Bison smoking and chatting over the old-times when there was a lot more shooting and killing, so it was alleged.

While the conversation was going on between those wild men about Hawkeye Hank and Horse Soldier, he was standing behind a door listening intently. Like his bartender he had heard the whole of the exchange between those desperadoes. That was why he had crept around the side of the saloon to listen when Tod Ridelle

went out to meet Yellow Tail. Everyone knew Yellow Tail was a drunk and had been a good tracker in his time. So this confirmed what Jack Logan had already heard.

In the next five minutes he was in Sheriff Ames's office.

'How yer doing?' the sheriff greeted as he rose to meet him. Ames was more portly than Sheriff Wills and his face was as prickly as a cactus because he never shaved too close.

'I just heard a conversation,' Jack Logan said.

Ames's eyebrows shot up. 'We all hear conversations from time to time, Jack,' he said.

'Sure, sure, but this one kind of worried me.' He sat down and told Ames what he had heard in the saloon and what Tod Ridelle and Yellow Tail had been discussing under the ramada.

Sheriff Ames listened with a serious expression on his face. Then he nodded. 'I hear what you say, Jack.

What d'you want for me to do about these men?'

Jack Logan looked about the office like he expected the three men in question to follow him in with their guns drawn. 'I fear a crime is about to be committed,' he said.

Sheriff Ames considered the matter. 'What d'you want me to do, lock them up in the jail?'

Jack Logan screwed up his face. 'Maybe we should try to stop this thing, Sheriff, before it gets out of control. There's liable to be a deal of shooting and people are going to be killed.'

Sheriff Ames considered the matter further. Then he shook his head. 'Sweet Spring is way out of my territory, Jack. I can't mess with the things that might or might not happen up there.'

Jack Logan wasn't happy. He was expecting visitors from the East in a couple of days. Rowdyism of any sort could be bad for trade.

'Tell you what you do,' Sheriff Ames said. 'Why don't you ride over to Little

Butte, tell Wills what you heard. Sweet Spring is closer to Little Butte. Wills might be inclined to take some kind of action.'

Jack Logan got up and looked out into the street. 'I might just do that,' he said.

* ★ *

Laramie Pete had his gun trained on Charlie Silversmith. Charlie stopped right where he was and awaited developments. As always his big moon face was smiling.

'Nice piece of horseflesh you got here,' Laramie Pete said in his deep voice. 'What you doin' around this clapped out town?'

'Just riding by,' Charlie said.

Laramie Pete didn't look too impressed. 'Just riding by.' He shook his head. 'You just riding by, how come you left your horse out here and came in real quiet on foot?' he asked.

Charlie was still smiling. 'Maybe I

wanted to look around, see if there was a chance to do a little trading,' he said.

Laramie Pete kept his gun on Charlie. 'Trading's good. Creeping up is another thing again. What do you have to trade?'

'Not much,' Charlie agreed. 'I make things with silver.'

Laramie Pete nodded and his rugged face cracked in a grin. 'Silver is good too. You got silver to trade?'

Charlie opened his hands to show he had nothing. 'I don't have silver with me. I make from silver. That's all.'

Laramie Pete was in two minds but he kept his Colt pointing in Charlie's direction. 'Maybe you should come along into the saloon with me. Have a drink. Maybe we could do some kind of deal.'

Charlie didn't like the sound of that. He could see his horse grazing on the sparse foliage beyond Laramie Pete and wondered how he could steer round the man with the gun in his hand and ride away intact.

Just at that moment Handsome Johnny came out from the back entrance of the saloon. He was lighting up a quirly when he looked up and saw Charlie and Laramie Pete with a gun on him.

'What the hell?' he said. He was laughing and his laugh wasn't friendly. 'What did you find here, Pete?'

Laramie Pete stepped forward. 'I found this Indian hanging around.'

'Well, now, this Indian don't look much like Yellow Tail to me.' Handsome Johnny stood a little to the right of Charlie. 'What you doing sneaking around here?' he said. 'You a friend of that drunk Yellow Tail?'

When you don't know what to say, it is best to keep quiet. That's what Charlie figured.

'Invited him in for a drink,' Laramie Pete said. 'Tells me he doesn't drink whiskey and can't abide beer.'

'Is that so?' Handsome Johnny jeered. 'Maybe you come inside and we find something you do like to drink. A

small whiskey with a deal of water. How would that be?'

Still Charlie said nothing. He was smiling but a puzzled look had come into his eyes.

Laramie Pete had stepped forward to stick the Colt into his ribs. 'You come inside and talk a little,' he said.

Charlie didn't protest He was starting to work out the best way to get free. He stepped into the clapped out saloon where Tod Ridelle was sitting at a table staring into his whiskey and wondering whether he could rely on Yellow Tail to lead them up to Sweet Spring. When he saw Charlie, he rose from the table and his twitch came on quite violently.

A voice came from the corner of the room. 'I'm sorry, gentleman, but we don't have no Indians in here. Tradition of the house.'

Tod Ridelle nodded. 'We must show respect for the house, boys, don't we?'

Charlie turned. He would be glad to get out into the air again. As he walked on past Handsome Johnny and past

81

Laramie Pete he felt their hostility like a hot breath on his cheek. Laramie Pete still had his Colt in his hand as though he was reluctant to put it in its holster. As he walked on towards his horse Charlie felt them walking close behind him.

'Hold on there!' Handsome Johnny said. 'I think we need to have a little talk here.'

Charlie paused. He had heard the click of a shooter being cocked. He turned slowly to look at the men. Both Handsome Johnny and Laramie Pete had guns drawn on him. Two armed men against one man without a gun. Tod Ridelle was a little further back laughing at the scene.

Charlie took a slow breath. 'You want to say something?' he asked.

'Sure we want to say something,' Laramie Pete said. 'We want to know why you were sneaking up to the place like that, why you had your horse half hidden in the mesquite there?'

'Nice piece of horse flesh too,'

Handsome Johnny jeered. 'Deserves better treatment than that.'

Tod Ridelle chuckled. Not a friendly sound.

Charlie read the signs and knew he was in some danger. These two men with guns were in competition. They wanted to impress one another. The third *hombre* just stood back and egged them on. Not a nice trio to be with.

'You want to tell us why you were hanging around here?' Handsome Johnny said.

'A man I knew. I thought I saw him,' Charlie said.

'Thought you saw who?' Laramie Pete asked.

Charlie glanced to one side. 'Thought I saw Yellow Tail,' he said.

'Yellow Tail!' Handsome Johnny marvelled. 'Yellow Tail a friend of yours?'

Charlie shook his head slowly. He was still smiling but his smile was now more of a defensive grin. 'Just had a word to say to him,' he said.

Handsome Johnny and Laramie Pete

exchanged suspicious glances but it was Tod Ridelle who spoke next. 'Why would you want to talk to Yellow Tail?' he asked.

Charlie was swallowing hard getting ready to answer but that wasn't fast enough for Handsome Johnny. He gripped Charlie by the throat with his left hand and stuck his Colt almost into the Indian's face. 'Answer the man, Injun!' he shouted. 'Why would you talk to Yellow Tail?'

Charlie was one patient man. Though he was well known for his psychic powers he had his breaking point. When he felt Handsome Johnny's hand gripping his throat and smelled the whiskey on his breath his temper broke. He thrust the Colt away from his face and jammed his elbow into Handsome Johnny's face. Charlie was like a tower of flesh and muscle and Handsome Johnny fell right back on the ground. As he fell he fired his Colt and the bullet went right past Charlie's ear. Now Charlie was turning. He struck out with

his fist at Laramie Pete and caught him on the side of the jaw just below his left ear. Charlie's fist was like a hammer and that was some punch! Laramie Pete staggered back and blood and a broken tooth came gushing from of his mouth.

Charlie was a big man but he was quick, especially when he was in trouble. Before Handsome Johnny could get onto his feet or cock his pistol and while Laramie Pete was still staggering about, coughing up blood and spitting out what was left of another tooth, Charlie was halfway to where his horse was tethered in the mesquite. In another second he was in the saddle and ready to ride.

But Charlie hadn't reckoned on one thing. Maybe he should have lashed out at Tod Ridelle too. Ridelle might have had a face twitch and a semi-permanent grin but he was also a quick-fire grudge man and he knew how to shoot. As Charlie turned to ride away, Ridelle loosed two shots at him in quick succession. The first shot missed but the second shot caught Charlie high

and spun him round in the saddle. His horse bolted and the last Ridelle saw of Charlie was Charlie drooping on the horse's back with his head against the horse's neck.

'You get him?' Handsome Johnny asked.

'I got him.' Tod Ridelle examined his shooter and dropped it into its holster. 'Got him high up. Don't figure it'll be long before he drops off into the brush and lies there food for the buzzards and the coyotes.'

'Think we should go after him, make sure?' Handsome Johnny suggested.

Tod Ridelle sniggered. 'I don't think so. Leave him to his Indian gods. Let them take care of him,' he said.

4

As soon as Hawkeye Hank saw the two riders approaching, a warning bell sounded in his head. One of the riders was Nino, Meralito's younger sister, the other was Manuel who was no more than a boy.

Nino dismounted and stood before Meralito in some distress. Meralito went to her and put her arms around her. Hawkeye Hank waited expectantly as they spoke quickly in Navajo. The boy Manuel looked on impassively.

'It's Charlie,' Meralito said. 'Charlie's missing. He went out riding two days ago. Didn't come back.'

Nino turned to her brother-in-law anxiously.

'Charlie doesn't always come back,' Hawkeye Hank said. 'Sometimes he stays away for a week. So that doesn't figure.'

Hawkeye Hank spoke to reassure the women, but he knew it wasn't strictly true. Sure, Charlie had been known to go missing for a week. Everyone knew Charlie was a dreamer, a seer, and a wanderer; he often went off to remember his old vision quest days. Everyone knew that. But Hawkeye Hank knew things were different this time. He sensed it deep in his bones.

Meralito had been restless lately too. She had had bad dreams ever since Jude Riverwind had shown up at the place. Sometimes she got up during the night and went to the door of the hogan and looked out restlessly at the glittering stars.

'You don't need to worry about me,' Hawkeye Hank had said. 'That Horse Soldier comes for me I'll be good and ready for him.'

Meralito shook her head. 'Not only about that,' she said. 'It's Charlie. I dreamed about him. The big eagle swooped down on him and clawed his shoulder. Right here,' she said, holding

her hand to her right shoulder. 'There was much blood. The big eagle wanted to carry Charlie away but Charlie held onto a boulder with his left hand. And the eagle left him to bleed. It rose up and landed on a mountain and waited.' Meralito paused as though she could still see the eagle perched on the mountain. She stretched out her hand and pointed. 'The eagle is still there waiting on that mountain looking down at Charlie.'

So it was no surprise when Nino and Manuel rode in. Nino also spoke about a dream she had had. In Nino's dream Charlie had been mauled and half eaten by a mountain lion. Charlie had beaten the big cat off and it now lay crouching on the mountainside waiting for Charlie to bleed to death. The same image in a different form.

Hawkeye Hank was not a man to panic easily but he knew about the Navajo and their dreams and he also knew that Charlie had unusual powers.

'I have to go find Charlie,' he said.

Easier said than done. Where could Charlie be in this big rugged country of bluffs, gullies, and ravines?

Manuel was staring intently at Hawkeye Hank. 'I will lead you to Charlie,' he said.

'You lead me to Charlie? How come?' Hawkeye Hank said. 'How do you know where Charlie is?'

Nino and Meralito were talking quietly together. Meralito turned to Hawkeye Hank. 'Manuel goes with Charlie everywhere. He is learning Charlie's skills. He understands the meaning of dreams. He will lead you there.'

Hawkeye Hank understood what Meralito was saying. The boy was a kind of understudy to Charlie. He was learning, not only the skills of hunting but the arts of medicine that Charlie had. The kid was being coached for his vision quest.

'You know where Charlie is right now?' he asked the boy.

Manuel looked puzzled for a moment.

Then he closed his eyes. He seemed to mutter to himself for a second. Then he nodded. 'I think I see him. He is close by a rock I know.'

Thinking is not knowing, Hawkeye Hank said to himself. He placed his hand on the boy's shoulder. 'Is Charlie in danger?'

The boy nodded. 'Charlie is wounded. He needs help. He needs you.' He spoke with such assurance that Hawkeye knew he had to act.

'So you think you can lead me there?'

'I lead you there,' Manuel said with confidence.

Hawkeye Hank didn't know what to make of that. But he did know one thing: if Charlie was in trouble he needed help and that was down to him. He turned to Meralito and she nodded.

'Go,' she said. 'Find Charlie and bring him back safe.'

So Hawkeye Hank took food and water and saddled up his horse.

'Nino will stay with me,' Meralito said.

'You look after that unborn child,' Hawkeye Hank said. 'And watch out for that Horse Soldier. You see him coming, you know where to hide. Keep right out of sight until he rides away, d'you hear me?'

'I hear you,' Meralito said.

Hawkeye Hank and the boy Manuel mounted up and started threading their way down the mountainside.

★ ★ ★

Horse Soldier rode high in the saddle and Jude Riverwind half slumped, looking right and left along the trail as though he was reading the signs. Why would Riverwind be reading the signs? Horse Soldier asked himself. That *hombre* knows the way to Sweet Spring without reading signs. There are no signs to read.

Maybe Jude Riverwind was taking him up a blind gulch for some reason.

'You looking for something?' Horse Soldier asked.

'Must look,' Jude Riverwind said. 'You never know what you could find.'

Horse Soldier didn't nod and he didn't smile. 'Like what kind of signs?' he said.

'Just signs on the trail,' Riverwind said.

Horse Soldier thought about that. He looked up into the west and saw that the sun was dancing low on the peaks. It would soon be time to make camp somewhere. The thought of spending the night out here with a man he couldn't trust didn't greatly appeal to him.

He reined in his horse. 'How much further?' he asked.

Jude Riverwind raised his head and sniffed the air. 'One hour, maybe two.'

'You sure we're on the right trail?'

Riverwind chuckled. 'No trail,' he said. 'You read the signs, watch the lie of the land, you get there. I show you a good place where you can gun down on Hawkeye Hank.'

No need to gun down, Horse Soldier

thought. Better to ride in, reason with the man, and take him in. That's the way it usually works. When a man knows it's death or surrender, he usually comes quietly. He took a bottle of Mad Jim's whiskey out of his saddle-bag and had a swig.

Jude Riverwind gave him a suspicious look. 'What do you do?' he asked.

'What we do,' Horse Soldier said, 'is we take our horses into this gulch and wait till sunup. You double-cross me we pull the blinds down and it's curtains for you.'

Jude Riverwind was grinning. 'There's no double-crossing here. You do what you have to do. I get my part of the reward.'

★   ★   ★

They found Yellow Tail under the sidewalk, pretending to be asleep. He was old and soft in the head but he wasn't quite as crazy as they thought. He had looked out from somewhere

close and seen the confrontation between Laramie Pete and Charlie Silversmiith. Charlie Silversmith was no friend of Yellow Tail and Yellow Tail knew it. But what happened to Charlie could happen to anybody, especially with a man like Handsome Johnny who enjoyed seeing people suffer and squirm.

'You been lying out here through the night?' Tod Ridelle said, prodding the Indian with the toe of his boot.

'Just taking a nap,' Yellow Tail grinned. 'Waiting on you guys.'

This old Indian stinks like hell, Tod Ridelle thought.

'Where d'you get this pile of horse shit?' Handsome Johnny said. He was feeling none too happy after the contact with Charlie's elbow which had given offence to his pride as well as his chest. Laramie Pete wasn't too happy either. His jaw was red and swollen where Charlie's hammer-like fist had made contact with it.

'OK,' Tod Ridelle said. 'We hit the

road, we'll be there before sundown.'

They mounted up, three men on horseback and an old Indian on a mule. Could have been one Sancho Panza riding with three Don Quixotes but none of them would see that comparison.

'See those buzzards circling up there?' Handsome Johnny said, pointing towards the mountains. 'That must be where that big Indian fell. Probably picking his bones clean and white.' He laughed.

Tod Ridelle's face twitched. 'I got him right,' he boasted. 'You know that Indian?' he asked Yellow Tail.

'I seen him,' Yellow Tail admitted. 'No friend to me.' Yellow Tail didn't say what was in his mind. Though he had no love for Charlie Silversmith, the picture of him lying out there having his bones picked clean didn't appeal to him one little bit. He rode on, wondering what to do. Maybe he should have made a break for it when he saw what happened to Charlie. Whiskey was one

thing; having your bones picked clean by buzzards was something else entirely.

★ ★ ★

Sheriff Wills was no ordinary lawman. He had respect for the law and for the job. When Jack Logan stepped into his office he showed no surprise. 'Why, Jack,' he said, 'what brings you to this neck of the woods and how are things doing in Hopeful?'

Jack Logan sat down in a chair across from the sheriff and Wills poured him a beer. 'I got three ornery *hombres* staying in the place,' he said. 'Happened to overhear a conversation just the other day and that conversation worried me.'

He told Wills what he had heard between the three men, including the part with Yellow Tail. When Sheriff Wills heard the name Yellow Tail his eyebrows slanted. Everyone knew Yellow Tail was bad medicine. He had spent a deal of

time in the calaboose and once he had shot a man to death. He would do almost anything for a bottle of bad whiskey.

But there was more. Logan told the sheriff about how those desperadoes had shot Charlie Silversmith and how they were about to pull out and head for the mountains and probably for Sweet Spring.

Sheriff Wills looked out towards the mountains. He knew they were strictly beyond his jurisdiction. Yet his conscience fretted him. He had heard stories about George James alias Hawkeye Hank, the white lawbreaker who had turned Indian. He had read the posters offering $5,000 for him dead or alive. But that was over the border in Texas. Why not let those dogs sleeping in the hot sun lie down and take their ease? Hawkeye Hank had got sort of respectable and that spoke well for a man even if he had committed a crime five years back in another state.

Another thing: the sheriff knew

Meralito, Hawkeye Hank's Navajo woman. The sheriff's own wife Maria purchased blankets and rugs from Meralito and sold them on. They had a good working relationship.

'Meralito crafts those blankets real well,' Maria Wills had said. 'I don't know anyone who crafts them better.'

Wills had run those Navajo blankets through his fingers and felt their quality and seen their bold patterning, and he had to agree.

'Have you told my friend Ames about these happenings?' he asked Logan.

Jack Logan held his head on one side. 'You know what Ames is like. He referred the whole thing to you. Said Sweet Spring was more in your territory than his.' He paused. 'You see, Sheriff, I fear a crime is about to be committed up there in the mountains and I don't want to have it on my conscience.'

Sheriff Wills turned the whole thing over in his mind. 'OK, Jack,' he said, 'why don't you leave this with me? I'll

see what I need to do.'

Jack Logan said his goodbyes and left to talk to a few acquaintances in the town.

Wills was still thinking things over when Maria came into the office. 'You surely can't interfere in this matter,' she said. 'Those Navajo can take care of themselves. It's none of our business.'

Now Wills had filled his pipe. He always smoked when he wanted to solve a problem.

Maria Wills wasn't done. 'Logan said they shot Charlie Silversmith. You know Charlie. Smiles all the time. He's a real craftsman. He's part of our future business too. Why would anyone want to shoot Charlie?'

Wills knew about Charlie Silver-smith. He'd seen him around Little Butte from time to time and admired his delicate silver-work.

'That's a real shame about Charlie,' Maria said. 'But you can't get tangled in this matter. You're way too old to get involved with gunmen and killers.

About time you retired from the law business. We have to think about our future, the store we plan to open up.'

Maria had a point, Wills had to agree to that. He had mixed feelings about Hawkeye Hank and Horse Soldier and bad feelings about the three gunmen riding out of Hopeful. One thing that really stuck in the sheriff's craw was injustice. The picture of three *hombres* riding in from one direction and Horse Soldier riding in from another direction to collect a reward on a man who was living peaceably at Sweet Spring didn't seem right to him.

So, as Maria rattled on, he was taking down shotguns and Winchesters from the rack and checking they were in good working order.

'You going some place?' Maria said.

Sheriff Wills grinned. 'Hunting trip,' he said. 'Thought I'd take a little time out. Could be away a few days.'

Maria nodded. She had heard that story before. One time her husband had been absent for a week on the trail of

some saddle bum threatening to burn people's homes down. You never knew with Wills. When he got some crazy idea in his head, it buzzed around like a troublesome fly before it settled. No use arguing with a man who was as stubborn as a mule.

'Just as long as you don't have an appointment with the angels,' she said. 'Those spirit beings have a habit of wanting to keep you to themselves once you get close to them. They're greedy that way.'

Sheriff Wills chuckled as he checked his Colt revolver. 'Send you a message by smoke signal when I get there,' he said.

He rode down to the Barren Rocks with a clear idea of what he had to do. Maria was right about one thing: he had no pension and no prospects for the future. Some time, and probably sooner rather than later, he must step down as sheriff. That might mean selling Navajo crafts to Eastern tourists which wasn't particularly attractive to an ex-man of the law. And $5,000 was

no mean sum either. Wills felt the Devil breathing close to his neck and the Devil said: those dollars would set you up really fine. You could move and purchase a store for Maria to go into business. She had the makings of a good business woman, and swinging back and forth in a rocking-chair had its appeal too. No more sheriff's star. No more six shooters. No more drunks and killers to think about. Maybe he deserved that easier life.

Wills had a keen sense of smell. He could smell a crime from a hundred miles away and this one stank real bad!

★   ★   ★

When he dismounted and walked into the Barren Rocks the place was as quiet as a Pharaoh's tomb, except for the occasional rustling of Mad Jim's out-of-date newspaper.

Mad Jim lowered it cautiously and stared out like a short sighted scarecrow. 'Why Sheriff Wills,' he said.

'Didn't think to see you so soon.'

'Give me a beer, will you?' the sheriff said. 'It's gonna be a hot day.'

Mad Jim reached up and drew him off a beer. 'New barrel in, day afore yesterday,' he said.

The sheriff sipped his beer and then drank it back in one gulp. 'What happened to that Horse Soldier *hombre?*' he said. 'Is he still around?'

'Oh, no. Horse Soldier pulled out yesterday.' Mad Jim spread his newspaper on the table and gave a high-pitched giggle. 'Hardly never seen anyone who could drink so much whiskey afore. Even poured it on his breakfast and topped up his coffee with it. Must have a gut made of cast iron.' He sniggered again.

'Ride out alone?' Sheriff Wills asked.

'No, no, no.' Mad Jim waved his arm about. 'Jude Riverwind rode with him. They fixed to ride out together.'

'You know why?' the sheriff asked him.

'Well, you know, Sheriff, I keep

myself to myself. So it's no never mind to me. Except . . . ' He raised his head slowly and met the sheriff's gaze.

'Except what?' Wills asked him.

'Except that she — that's my woman Sarah — she says Riverwind aims to lead Horse Soldier up to Sweet Spring. They struck a deal on that.'

Wills looked at the wall where most of the Wanted notices were pasted and saw a blank space where the wanted notice for Hawkeye Hank had been.

'I see a space where that wanted notice was pasted,' he said.

'You see right.' Mad Jim nodded. 'Horse Soldier did that. He just reached up and took it down, real neat and respectful like he was honouring a dear friend or something. Guess he wanted to make sure of his identification. You bring a man in, you got to be damned sure it's the right one, don't you?'

Sheriff Wills had to agree to that. He placed his glass on the table and got up slowly. 'Give my best regards to Sarah,' he said.

'You stick around, Sarah might fix you some lunch,' Mad Jim offered.

'Thanks for the offer,' Wills said. 'I got other things on my mind.' He moved to the door and turned. 'Sorry I couldn't stay longer. I got work to do.'

He went outside and mounted up. He didn't need to do much tracking. He knew full well which way led in the direction of the mountains and Sweet Spring and it wasn't long before he picked up the recent trail of the two riders.

★ ★ ★

As Hawkeye Hank and the boy rode on, Hawkeye Hank became increasingly sceptical about Manuel's ability to engage with Charlie's mind and home in on where he lay. The boy drew in suddenly and pointed away to the east where a cloud of buzzards were circling. 'Look, that's where Charlie lies.'

Buzzards were a bad sign. Either there was meat to be torn apart and

devoured or they were waiting to drop down for the kill. Either way it didn't look good.

It began to look even worse when they rode on and found Charlie's horse. It was standing amidst a stand of low junipers. As they approached, it raised its head and waited for a moment, then it came ambling towards them. No question: that horse knew Manuel. Thought of him as a friend.

Manuel and Hawkeye Hank dismounted. Manuel caught the horse's rein and whispered reassuring words. The horse's ears twitched and it shook its head.

Hawkeye Hank ran his hand down the horse's flank. 'Lookee here,' he said, 'there's blood on the saddle.'

There was matted blood, quite a lot of it.

'Someone shot Charlie,' the boy said. He took the horse's reins and mounted up. 'Now we find Charlie.'

Maybe Charlie's dead, Hawkeye Hank thought. Things don't look good.

But finding the horse gave Manuel renewed confidence. Now they could follow the horse's tracks back along the trail and find Charlie, dead or alive.

Manuel had learned a lot from Charlie and, as they rode, he leaned over and read the signs. Charlie's horse seemed content to trot back too, like he was pleased to show the way.

They found Charlie lying facing the sky as though he had confronted death nobly and was looking towards the place where the old chiefs were waiting in the sky. The buzzards were circling low. One or two were already on the ground waiting like the grim guardians of death.

They screeched and took off when Hawkeye Hank sprang down from the saddle and the boy knelt beside Charlie and raised his head. 'I think Charlie's dead,' he moaned.

Hawkeye Hank stooped close peering into the dead face. Something in Charlie's features twitched and his eyes opened quickly and closed again.

'Steady there,' Hawkeye Hank said. 'Get a blanket and cover him. Gather brush and light up a fire.'

The boy needed no bidding. Charlie had taught him all he knew about survival.

Under the blanket Charlie lay like a sculpture without a breath. Just once in a while the air came out of his lungs in a slow gasp.

'We got to get that bullet out of his chest,' Hawkeye Hank said.

The boy already had a knife on a stone on the fire to cleanse it.

'No whiskey,' Hawkeye Hank muttered to himself. 'We gotta do this without the aid of deadening.' He leaned over Charlie. 'Listen, Charlie, can you hear me speaking to you?'

Charlie seemed to come out of a deep dream. His eyes flickered open and he gave a slight nod.

'That's good,' Hawkeye Hank said. 'Now I'm going to ask you to open your mouth and take this hickory stick between your teeth. You bite on it and I

gouge out that slug. You understand me, boy?'

Charlie nodded slowly.

'That's good.'

Hawkeye Hank offered the hickory stick up to Charlie's mouth and Charlie clamped his teeth tight on it.

'Now this is gonna hurt some,' Hawkeye Hank said. 'You hear me?'

Charlie nodded and clamped harder.

Hawkeye Hank had respect for Charlie. Respect and deep love. He knew that when a man is in agony he might fall into such wildness that he might hurl himself and those who were nursing him right on the fire. The boy was too young and too weak to hold Charlie down. Yet he held his arm and pushed hard.

Charlie groaned and his eyes opened wildly.

'Steady there, steady,' Hawkeye Hank whispered as he held the knife over the place where the bullet had entered Charlie's chest. Either this is going to kill him or save his life, he thought. He

nodded at the boy and made the incision.

Charlie was one brave man. When the knife entered his shoulder, he shuddered and clenched his teeth on the hickory stick. Hawkeye Hank felt him starting to buck and rear under the knife. But Charlie held himself rigid and kept himself under control. That is some brave Navajo, Hawkeye Hank thought.

5

Hawkeye Hank was kneeling over Charlie and peering at him intently. Charlie seemed to be in a deep sleep, though his big round face twitched spasmodically from time to time.

'We got here just about right,' Hawkeye Hank said. 'Got that slug out good and clean. Now it's a matter of waiting.'

They had covered the wound with healing herbs that the boy Manuel knew about.

'Can't move Charlie till he gets some of his strength back,' Hawkeye Hank muttered to himself. He turned to Manuel. 'Listen, I want for you to do something.'

The boy held up his hand as though he was about to take an oath.

Hawkeye Hank nodded. 'I want for you to ride back to Sweet Spring. Tell

Meralito and Nino we found Charlie. Tell them he is too sick to move right now but we think he's going to be all right. Can you do that?'

'I do that,' the boy said.

Hawkeye Hank stood up. He put his hand on Manuel's should. 'Take it easy. Ride carefully. Don't take any risks. Whoever shot Charlie might be still around somewhere. Right now we've got to look after Charlie. Then we find out who did this, and . . . ' Hawkeye Hank made a gesture like a knife chopping through flesh.

The boy nodded. He looked down at Charlie for a moment and then mounted up and rode away.

Hawkeye Hank leaned over the wounded man and made strange keening noises as if to lure him back from the world of the spirits.

'You're gonna be OK, buddy,' he said. 'You're gonna be OK.' It was more of a wish than a promise.

★ ★ ★

Come sunup Tod Ridelle was ready to hit the trail. Handsome Johnny was rolling up his bedroll. He had taken a stroll in among the mesquite and juniper and was looking about restlessly. Handsome Johnny could never keep still for a second. He had a taste for action, good or bad; it didn't much matter what it was. Bad action was often more fulfilling.

Laramie Pete had yet to stir out of his bedroll. He had his hat pulled down over his eyes and you might have said he was asleep. But Laramie Pete never slept for long or too easily. You could see from the cast of his brow and his craggy features that he was the worrying kind. He was worrying now about the wisdom of killing that Indian Charlie. Other things too. That Eldorado gold Tod Ridelle kept dangling before them; Laramie Pete had real doubts about that gold. Did it really exist, or not? Or was it a mere figment of Tod Ridelle's fevered brain? Tod Ridelle was a grudge man and a grudge

man can get you into a deal of trouble with his fantasies.

'Chow up!' Tod Ridelle crowed suddenly. He started banging on a a tin plate with a spoon, and that jarred against Laramie Pete's ears too. First thing in the morning was not a good time for a worrying man like Laramie Pete.

Handsome Johnny was flexing his muscles on the edge of the camp. He had real pride in his physique. Had thought of being a boxer once. So, he had stripped off his shirt, found a pool and thrown cold water over his head and face and chest to wake himself up. 'You got chow?' he said. Then he sang out '*All God's people got chow*!' Handsome Johnny thought he had a fine tenor voice, but that wasn't the way Laramie Pete heard it. To him it sounded like an old prairie chicken clucking out its death rattle.

'Why don't you shut that noise?' he barked out from under his hat.

Handsome Johnny laughed and pretended not to be offended, but Laramie Pete had the uncanny knack of pressing his finger on the sore spot. To make matters worse, Handsome Johnny squinted down the sights of his Smith & Wesson and fired off a couple of shots into the brushwood sending a whole bunch of birds clucking and squawking into the morning air. The sound of the shots went echoing and bouncing all down the gullies and canyons, right to the end of the world . . . or so it seemed.

Laramie Pete sat bolt upright and grabbed his shooter. 'Wassat?' he said.

Handsome Johnny laughed, twirled his Smith & Wesson and slid it into its holster. 'Keep your pants on, big man,' he said. 'Just practising for the great day when I can take out that Hawkeye Hank.'

Tod Ridelle struck the tin plate again and the rather tattered figure of Yellow Tail emerged from close by. Yellow Tail kept himself to himself, not because he

was particular but because he had no appetite for being shot as he had seen Charlie Silversmith shot.

Yellow Tail had thought about sliding away during the night. It would have been easy. He could have cut out the horses and ridden them off. Horses would fetch a good price, even enough to keep a fellow in booze for a month or more. But Yellow Tail would bide his time and watch out for any opportunities that came his way. He might look half crazed but he kept his eyes peeled and he still had a good share of cunning.

After food it was time to take a council of war and Tod Ridelle felt his responsibility. 'This is the day,' he said when they had saddled up their horses.

'What day is that?' Handsome Johnny enquired mischievously.

Tod Ridelle fancied himself as a politician, thought he might be in the government some day. 'I mean the day of vengeance and reward,' he said. 'My vengeance and your reward.'

Laramie Pete gave him a long craggy look. He was still smarting about Handsome Johnny's pranks. 'We got to be practical about this,' he suggested. 'From what I hear this Hawkeye Hank might be quite a handful. A man isn't called Hawkeye for nothing. Stands to reason.'

'Just so long as I get some gun play,' Handsome Johnny said. 'When the time comes, I get to shoot Hawkeye Hank.'

'You get your cut,' Tod Ridelle said. 'I get to shoot Hawkeye Hank. That's a matter of honour after what he did to my brother and for the gold Hawkeye Hank stole from him which is rightfully mine. We've got to make that galloot tell us where that gold is hidden first off.'

Handsome Johnny laughed and Laramie Pete looked glum.

'We'll see how things pan out,' he said.

'What about that booze you promise?' Yellow Tail suddenly interjected.

Tod Ridelle gave him a quick quizzical look. 'You get all the booze

you can hold and some over if you lead us up to that place where Hawkeye Hank is nested. There's gonna be enough and more for everybody.'

Laramie Pete was still not convinced. 'Then how come we never took this road before?' he asked. 'Could be easier robbing banks or stages, or even the railroad.'

Tod Ridelle raised his head and sniffed the air. 'Listen, Pete,' he said. 'I been on this trail ever since my brother got cheated and killed. You're with me, that's good. You want out, you do it. It's your call.'

'Like the three musketeers!' Handsome Johnny chuckled.

'Who the hell are they?' Laramie Pete growled.

'All for one and one for all,' Handsome Johnny explained. 'I read it in a book once. At least someone else read it to me. They call it loyalty, Pete. You never hear of loyalty?'

'I heard about royalty,' Laramie Pete said laconically. 'I believe they have it in

Europe somewhere, so they tell.'

'Just let us get up to that Sweet Spring,' Tod Ridelle said. 'Then we can discuss royalty.'

★   ★   ★

Jude Riverwind was riding just ahead of Horse Soldier. Horse Soldier rode a horse's length behind. He had just taken a quick swig from his whiskey bottle when he heard the shots from way off to the right. They were faint and, if he hadn't paused to gulp down his whiskey he wouldn't have heard them. He reined in his mount to listen for more. Riverwind had stopped too. He had the keen hearing of an Indian and he could read what he heard. These shots were borne on the wind and funnelled down the gulch from higher ground. Not hunting rifles but side-arms, he figured.

'How d'you read that?' Horse Soldier asked him.

Jude Riverwind sniffed the air. He

was learning to respect Horse Soldier as well as fear him. He knew well that anyone who tried to cross Horse Soldier could be in danger of lying dead before he could count to ten.

'Not hunters,' he said. 'Hunting rifles don't sound that way.'

'What do you figure?' Horse Soldier pressed.

Jude Riverwind couldn't answer that. He felt jumpy already and the sound of those shots made him feel even more nervous. He wasn't a man of imagination but he had enough to picture a whole posse of men riding out to apprehend him and Horse Soldier.

'How much further to Sweet Spring?' Horse Soldier asked.

'A short distance. Easy riding,' said Jude Riverwind. He was beginning to wonder what he had got himself into. What could he say to Hawkeye Hank? What might Meralito do?

Horse Soldier nodded. 'Listen up,' he said.

'I'm listening good,' Jude Riverwind.

'When we get to Sweet Spring, you do what I tell you,' Horse Soldier said. 'No false moves. We don't want any unnecessary killings here, do we?'

'No, sir,' Riverwind said. This whole thing might be a deal more complicated than I thought, he figured. 'Just as long as I get my reward,' he said.

Horse Soldier gave a low chuckle, more like a growl.

★   ★   ★

The boy Manuel was on the trail back to Sweet Spring when he heard the shots that Handsome Johnny had loosed off.

He was quite close to where Tod Ridelle and his bunch were striking camp. He knew he could edge in and see the three white gringos and the Indian and check what they were doing. But Manuel was torn between two actions. He wanted to get back to Sweet Spring and tell Meralito and Nino what had happened to Charlie. The one thing

122

uppermost in his mind was that he and Hawkeye had to save Charlie's life. The question was, if he got back to Sweet Spring would it do anything to help Charlie?

Manuel gave in to temptation. He dismounted and led his pony as close as he could to where the bunch were striking camp. He crouched and watched as the three men gathered their goods together and mounted up. Manuel had a bad feeling about those three *hombres* striking camp. He had heard rumours among the tribe that some white *hombres* were in the area possibly looking for trouble. When you saw an Indian like Yellow Tail you knew trouble was never very far away. Yellow Tail lived and drank trouble. Yellow Tail was bad medicine. What was Yellow Tail doing riding on the trail with these three *hombres*? Manuel put two and two together and its wasn't difficult to make four. He crept back through the brush, mounted his pony, and rode on as

fast as he could towards Sweet Spring.

But Manuel was in too much of a hurry. He forgot to keep his usual weather eye on the trail and he didn't see the rattlesnake until it had arced up and struck his pony high on the leg. The pony whinnied and reared suddenly in panic and Manuel was thrown back onto the rocks. He struck his head on an outcrop of rock and was knocked out cold. He lay for a time like a dead man and then shook his head suddenly and sat up. It could have been worse, he thought. That rattler might have struck again and taken me out.

He got to his feet slowly and shook his legs. In spite of the persistent buzzing in his head, he was still alive. He looked around but his pony was nowhere to be seen. Was it grazing somewhere not too far away, or was it lying poisoned and dead?

Manuel had nothing but the knife on his belt and his wits. He had let himself down and let Hawkeye Hank down too

And above all he had let Charlie down. What would Charlie think of him? What would he want of him? Should he walk back to Hawkeye Hank and Charlie, or continue on to Sweet Spring and warn Meralito and Nino about what had happened to Charlie and what Yellow Tail and those three white gringos might have in mind?

After considering for a moment, he turned his face towards the mountains and began the long trek towards Sweet Spring.

★ ★ ★

Meralito and Nino knew that something was wrong. Time was passing and Hawkeye Hank and the boy hadn't returned. Nino knew in her bones that something had happened to Charlie. The two women knew something else too. Meralito was close to her time. The longer they waited the closer it came. Meralito was getting restless. She had the urge to sweep out the hogan and

tidy up and sort things out before the baby arrived.

Nino observed all this and she knew she couldn't leave Meralito.

'Sister,' she said, 'we have to make a decision. That coming child needs to be taken care of.'

'I know that, Nino,' Meralito said irritably, 'but I'm worried about Hawk-eye and Charlie.'

Nino shook her head. 'They have to care for themselves, Meralito. Hawkeye and the boy know what they're doing. We have to think of you and the child.' It was a brave thing to say. Nino had a strong bond with both of those men, and Charlie in particular. 'My opinion is we should go back to our own people right now, so you can have your baby up there. I know Hawkeye would want that.'

Meralito thought of the old-times when having a child wasn't considered a big deal. Those old Navajo women had sometimes had their babies on the trail. Like the ancient buffalo herds they

had to keep moving in case the wolves attacked them. That was before the Navajo people settled in the Chelly Canyon and started to grow peaches and before Colonel Kit Carson came to defeat them and rob them of their land and their inheritance.

Meralito was in a dilemma. She knew Nino was right but she couldn't bring herself to leave the hogan even if her time was close.

★ ★ ★

Jude Riverwind and Horse Soldier were quite close. Horse Soldier was still riding a little behind Riverwind and Riverwind felt the hair pricking on the back of his neck.

'How far?' Horse Soldier asked from close behind.

'Pretty close,' Riverwind said. 'We stop right here. Climb up on this flat rock and you can see.'

Horse Soldier nodded and they tethered their horses.

'You go first,' Horse Soldier ordered.

Jude Riverwind climbed up on the rock and spread-eagled himself against it. He was trying to think of a way to get out of this situation, but every time he thought of a move his heart quivered and he wilted.

Horse Soldier climbed up and stretched out beside him. He produced a small telescope and laid it on the warm rock.

'Just right there.' Riverwind pointed. 'You see it good. That's the Sweet Spring,' he said.

Horse Soldier didn't need telling. It was obvious. He raised the telescope and focused it on the cascading water. 'So that's the Sweet Spring,' he muttered to himself.

'Very sweet,' Riverwind said. He knew this was the chance he had waited for. If he felt about with his hand he might find a loose rock that he could use to dash Horse Soldier on the side of the head before he knew what hit him.

Not so easy! There were no loose

rocks and this Horse Soldier had eyes everywhere. He also seemed to have an uncanny instinct about what another man was thinking.

In fact, Horse Soldier did know what was in Riverwind's mind and he also caught the stink of his fear in his nostrils. But he concentrated on that Sweet Spring and thought it looked good, the silver blue water cascading down the rocks and splashing into the pool below. A place where a man could strip off his clothes and float on his back, forgetting the cares of the world.

He panned to the left and saw the hogan and the two women sitting there. An ideal place, he thought, for a man to use as a hideaway. He wondered how long Hawkeye Hank had been holed up there, and for a moment he envied the man.

No sign of Hawkeye Hank. Maybe he had lit out for somewhere already.

He lowered the telescope and leaned on one elbow to consider his position.

'What you aim to do?' Jude Riverwind asked.

Horse Soldier nodded. 'What I aim is
this. We go in and parley with those
women. Ask them where Hawkeye
Hank is and how long he's likely to be
away. That's what we do.'

Riverwind moved his head from side
to side. 'I can't do that,' he said. 'That's
Meralito, Hawkeye's woman, and Nino
her sister. They put trust in me.'

'Sure they trust you. That's why
we're going to talk. We don't want to
spook the mares, do we?'

Riverwind continued shaking his
head. 'That wasn't part of the deal. You
said to show you Sweet Spring so you
give Hawkeye what you brought for
him. That was the deal.'

Horse Soldier's hand moved to the
butt of his Colt revolver. 'What we do is
you go right in and talk to those
women. That's what we do.'

Riverwind looked at Horse Soldier
and saw eyes as hard as pebbles staring
at him.

'I ride in first. You come in behind, keep your gun on me. That way they think I'm a prisoner. OK?'

Horse Soldier's lips curled in a smile. He was relentless and he was enjoying Riverwind's discomfort. 'If that's what you want,' he agreed. 'But remember what I said about false moves.'

Jude Riverwind elbowed his way down the flat rock.

They gathered the horses and mounted up. Riverwind rode on with a prickly feeling in his spine.

Horse Soldier rode easily in the saddle, keeping his shooter trained on Riverwind's back.

Riverwind gave a gloomy nod. 'What do I say to them?'

'You just say, this is a man wants to talk to Hawkeye Hank. Has something to give him. If Hawkeye is in that hogan I shall know what to do. If he isn't home, we find out where he's at. You understand me?'

Riverwind felt uneasy in his pants. He was still wondering how he had

131

been such a fool as to get himself into this situation as he rode on between the bluffs towards Sweet Spring.

★　★　★

Meralito saw the approaching riders before Nino. She grabbed the Winchester she kept by her side and jerked down the lever.

'Someone coming,' she said.

'That's Jude Riverwind!' Nino exclaimed. 'He's got company.'

'Company,' Meralito reflected, bringing the Winchester to her shoulder and training it on the man riding behind Riverwind. 'You keep right where you are!' she said.

The two riders reined in their mounts.

Meralito had never trusted Riverwind. Now his body language suggested something more than discomfort. She could see he was as scared as a spooked mustang. The other rider had a mask-like expression on his face which gave nothing away.

'Man told me to bring him here,' Jude Riverwind croaked. 'Says he has something to give Hawkeye.'

Horse Soldier nodded slightly and said nothing. His eyes roamed over the two women and he saw that the one holding the Winchester was close to her time. The other looked defiant too, but not quite as brave.

'Is Hawkeye Hank around?' Horse Soldier asked.

Meralito gestured with the Winchester. 'You got something for Hawkeye, you leave it right there. Turn around and ride out again. We don't welcome strangers.'

Horse Soldier was still grinning like a mask people wear at Halloween parties. 'What we've got for Hawkeye isn't the sort you can leave lying about on the ground,' he said.

Meralito's eyes turned to Jude Riverwind and she saw there was no help from him. Nino was shaking. So it was down to her. She motioned with the Winchester again.

'Hawkeye isn't here. So you'd better just go . . . '

Instead of backing off, Horse Soldier eased his mount forward a pace. 'Can you use that Winchester?' he said.

Yes, she can use it, he answered himself. She would use it to protect her man if she had to. Something to do with loyalty, he thought. Horse Soldier valued loyalty highly, that and dedication.

'Is that your work, ma'am?' he asked, with his eye on a blanket Meralito was weaving.

'That's what I do,' Meralito said. 'Weaving.'

Horse Soldier nodded. 'That's a real pretty blanket, ma'am. Mind if I take a closer look?'

Before Meralito could reply, he dismounted and strode up towards the hogan area. Meralito still had the Winchester trained on him, but he holstered his Colt and knelt down to examine the blanket more closely. 'This blanket is real pretty,' he said. 'You get much for it

when you sell it?'

Meralito shook her head. 'I sell them in Little Butte and other places. Sometimes someone sells them for me.'

'That so.' Horse Soldier fingered the blanket delicately. 'I like the design. You Navajo people have a rare gift in that.' He turned to Meralito. 'When do you expect Hawkeye back?' he asked.

The two women exchanged glances. Nino seemed about to speak, but Meralito gave a faint shake of the head. She was still holding the Winchester ready.

'He comes when he comes,' she said.

Horse Soldier gave her a hard unrelenting stare. 'Mind if I wait?'

Meralito shrugged. 'You wait he might never come back.'

Horse Soldier was grinning again. When he grinned under that dark hat he looked like a corpse risen from a recently dug grave.

Horse Soldier settled down on a stool with his legs stretched out. 'I have a

mind to wait,' he reiterated.

Jude Riverwind was still astride his horse. He looked bewildered. Couldn't make up his mind what to do. Horse Soldier was looking right at him. 'Go feed the horses,' he said, 'and give them good clean water to slake their thirsts. They've come a long way, those beasts. Always treat your horses good, they never let you down.'

Riverwind looked at Meralito and she ignored him. He dismounted and led the horses into the barn beside the water.

Horse Soldier produced his telescope and scanned the hills and the mountains beyond. 'Real nice place you got up here, ma'am,' he said.

Meralito grunted and disappeared into the hogan. Nino stared at the interloper for a second and then followed.

* * *

The boy Manuel had climbed to a little peak he knew that overlooked the Sweet

Spring. It had been a long climb and he needed time to breathe. As he rested back on a rock, thinking about Charlie and Hawkeye Hank, he still wondered whether he had done the right thing leaving them back there. And he still cursed his own foolishness over the rattler and his horse. He had hoped the horse might make its way back to him, but he reckoned the poison had penetrated deep and the horse was lying dead out there being eaten by buzzards and coyotes. Manuel had seen buzzards circling all through his long walk. So he wasn't optimistic.

He was now close to Sweet Spring. He would just rest here a little to get back his breath. Then he would walk on and tell Meralito and Nino the news about Charlie. As he thought about that, he levered himself up and peered out in the direction of the Sweet Spring. He could see the hogan quite clearly. He could almost have reached out and touched it, the air was so clear. What he saw surprised him. No sign of

the two women. Just Jude Riverwind leading two horses into the barn. And then he saw another man scanning the hills and crags all round through a telescope.

Strange! He had never seen that man before.

As he watched, the man with the telescope brought it round to focus on him. It almost seemed that he had read his thoughts and knew he was there. As he watched, Horse Soldier rose from his stool and seemed to peer even more intently in his direction.

Manuel kept himself very still. Framed against the rocks surely nobody could possibly see him. Yet Horse Soldier continued looking for several more seconds before he panned away with the telescope to search in other directions.

Manuel's heart was pounding fast. What was this stranger doing at the Sweet Spring? Why had Jude Riverwind put those horses in the barn as though they were meant to be there?

6

The boy Manuel couldn't figure out what to do. He had seen Meralito and Nino disappearing into the hogan and the stranger sitting outside peering round with his telescope. When Jude Riverwind led the horses into the barn, it puzzled Manuel. Who could this inquisitive stranger be? Why should Jude Riverwind be made welcome at Sweet Spring? Everyone knew that Hawkeye Hank and Meralito had never liked Riverwind.

Manuel puzzled for a bit longer. Then he slid down from the rock and started back to where he had left Hawkeye Hank and Charlie. He figured he couldn't do much to help those two women but he might be able to warn Hawkeye about the man watching out by the hogan and the four men who were still some distance off riding

towards Sweet Spring.

It was a long trudge back along the trail but he kept to the high ground following his own tracks. A mile or two on he put his ear to the ground and heard the sound of horses approaching. They were advancing slowly. So he got off the trail and climbed into a stunted tree to wait.

What he saw surprised him: Hawkeye Hank came riding towards him and behind him Charlie Silversmith on his own horse. Charlie wasn't so much sitting in the saddle as lying forward against the horse's neck.

Manuel swung down from the tree and waved his arms at Hawkeye.

Hawkeye reined in and waited.

'How come you're here?' Hawkeye said.

The kid was embarrassed. In his own mind he'd been a fool to let that rattler strike his horse. But he had other more important things to say. He told Hawkeye about the three men on the trail with Yellow Tail and that he had

seen a stranger sitting in front of the hogan looking all round with a telescope. Hawkeye was listening intently. When the kid mentioned Jude Riverwind and the barn his face came up like a wolf listening to the distant baying of a rival pack.

'You say Meralito and Nino went into the hogan?' he said.

At the name Nino Charlie raised his head from the horse's neck. 'What happened to Nino?' he asked.

Charlie's wound was healing thanks to Manuel's compound, but the boy's mentor seemed very weak. Hawkeye had wanted to stay where they'd found Charlie until Charlie regained some of his strength, but Charlie had insisted on getting back into the saddle.

'Those two women need us,' he had said. 'I've seen a picture in my mind and I don't like it. We've got to get back there to protect them.'

'You bide still,' Hawkeye said. 'I think Meralito and Nino know what they must do.'

Charlie squinted at him over the horse's neck and then rested back again. Maybe, the two women would be OK. He was probably too weak to do anything to help them, anyway.

*   *   *

When Jude Riverwind came out of the barn he couldn't figure out what to do next. Horse Soldier was still there perching like some kind of predatory bird. He wasn't looking through his telescope. He had his hand on his Winchester. Riverwind couldn't see his eyes. He just felt them staring out at him from under the brim of that sinister looking Stetson.

'You feed them good?' Horse Soldier asked laconically.

'What we do now?' Riverwind asked.

'Like I said, we wait.'

'You wait till doomsday. Nobody will come. They see you setting there,' Riverwind said. 'You don't think Hawk-eye Hank is about to come in and give

himself up, do you?'

Horse Soldier nodded. 'He'll come if he knows we've got the two women. He won't know how to stop himself.'

Riverwind came closer. 'Point is we don't have the two women, do we?'

Horse Soldier looked at him sideways. 'Those women are inside the hogan. Maybe you'll be kind enough to invite them to come out and join us. Then Hawkeye Hank will see we're one big happy family.'

Riverwind shook his head. 'I don't think so.'

'Why don't you think so?' Horse Soldier said.

'I don't think so, because they go into that hogan they turn into nothing,' Riverwind said.

Horse Soldier swung his head towards the entrance of the hogan. Was this some kind of Indian hocus pocus? He got up from the stool.

'You walk right along ahead of me,' he said, 'and we bring those squaws out here.'

Jude shrugged, pulled aside the skin covering the hogan entrance, and went inside, Horse Soldier following close behind. It was dim but not completely dark. There was an oil lamp on a slab of stone which partly revealed the interior, pots and pans and other hardware neatly arranged by a woman's hand. But no women.

Horse Soldier drew his Colt and explored the room. Right at the back was another skin curtain. He moved towards it and drew it back. What he saw was the entrance to a cave but those two women had vanished!

Horse Soldier let the curtain drop into place again. He went to the entrance to the hogan and peered out, gun in hand. Then he turned. River-wind was standing close by the entrance to the cave looking kind of self satisfied.

'Told you they would disappear, didn't I?' he said.

Horse Soldier nodded and grinned. 'Tell you what you do. You go right in

after them. Talk to them real nice and polite. Tell them to come out here, no harm intended. That's what you do.'

Riverwind shrugged again. He had no wish to go into that creepy network of caves. A man could get lost in there. There were plenty of Navajo stories about men who disappeared and found their way out a hundred years later with no flesh on their bones. The ghosts of ancestors too. Those women must be crazy!

Horse Soldier gestured with his Colt. 'Go on, go in there. Be polite. Tell them Horse Soldier is getting lonely. He wants their company. Wants to take a look at a few more Indian rugs. Might want to do a deal.' He gestured with the Colt again.

Jude turned towards the cave entrance again. Then he stooped and ventured into the dark interior.

$\star$ $\star$ $\star$

'That's the place up there!' Yellow Tail pointed up the mountain and Tod

Ridelle saw the blue-white spume of water cascading down.

'Yes, that's it,' he said.

'You want for me to ride ahead and flush that Hawkeye out?' Handsome Johnny said.

'Don't be dumb,' Laramie Pete growled. 'Time comes we all go in together.'

'That's right,' Tod Ridelle said. He looked up at the distant hogan.

A man emerged from behind the curtain and stepped out into the sun. He had a gun in his hand and he was looking round as though expecting visitors.

Yellow Tail screwed up his eyes. 'That not Hawkeye Hank,' he said.

'What d'you mean that's not Hawkeye Hank?' Handsome Johnny said. 'You sure this is the right place?'

'Right place sure,' Yellow Tail said. 'I know Sweet Spring. That's not Hawkeye Hank.'

'Whoever he is looks like he's expecting visitors,' Laramie Pete said.

Tod Ridelle looked thoughtful. 'I have a hunch that's Horse Soldier,' he said.

Laramie Pete leaned forward and shaded his eyes. 'Sure, that's Horse Soldier,' he said. 'That means he got ahead of us. He's waiting for Hawkeye Hank. Could be tricky.'

Handsome Johnny was laughing quietly to himself. 'That gives us the advantage,' he said. 'We see him. He don't see us. We sneak up and take him out. Nothing to it.'

'That nothing to it could cost you your life,' Laramie Pete grunted. 'You sneak up on a snake you have to know where to grab it. Snake bite can be fatal.'

That caused food for thought.

'We move in on three sides we can gun him down easy,' Handsome Johnny suggested. 'He's setting out there like a clay pigeon asking to be shot.'

'That Horse Soldier is no clay pigeon,' Laramie Pete said. 'He's quicker than devil lightning. You think

147

he's asleep he's just waiting to strike at you.'

Tod Ridelle said nothing. He was trying to figure out their best move. He wanted Hawkeye Hank and the gold. Horse Soldier was a rival and an obstacle.

Then, surprisingly, Yellow Tail piped up. 'You give me part of the reward dollars and some of that gold, I take that Horse Soldier out.'

The other three turned to look at him with contempt. 'You couldn't take out a prairie chicken if it was right under your crooked nose,' Handsome Johnny said.

Yellow Tail drew a long bowie knife and held it under Handsome Johnny's nose. Maybe Yellow Tail looked as though he spent most of his life crawling through the dust but that knife was gleaming, sharp, and deadly. 'I drop Horse Soldier with this. Be dead before he knows what hit him,' he declared.

Even Handsome Johnny looked impressed.

'You take Horse Soldier out you get your reward,' Tod Ridelle said. 'Just as long as I get revenge on that Hawkeye Hank.'

Before anything else could be said Yellow Tail slid down off his mule and disappeared behind a rock. He was more like a lizard than a man. Maybe that was why they called him Yellow Tail.

* * *

Meralito and Nino were well into the heart of the mountain by now. Behind the hogan there was an elaborate system of caves that branched out in every direction. A man or woman could easily get lost in that network but Meralito and Nino had known about them all their lives. Nino was carrying a flaming torch which sent out weird shadows on the greenish walls. Making your way through those caves was no picnic but the two women figured they had no option.

'We've got to get away from that evil

man,' Nino said. 'If he follows we can lose him. He could never find his way through here till the world ends.'

Meralito knew she was right: the skulls and bones of many dead men lay scattered in those caves. If you talked above a whisper your voice echoed away like the voices of long dead men calling from the other world. That's why even the bravest Navajo warriors avoided them.

'I'm not happy about this,' Meralito said. 'We leave that man Horse Soldier sitting there waiting for Hawkeye, he's going to kill him. I saw that in his eyes.'

'Would it be better if we were waiting there too?' Nino reasoned. 'Hawkeye knows what he's doing. He's no man to be caught by some bounty hunter.'

'Another thing,' Meralito said. 'We don't know what happened to Charlie, do we? We should have tried to warn them some way.'

Nino said, 'We still have a chance to do that. We get through this cave we can have a chance to do that.'

Meralito wasn't so sure. She knew there were places where you could look out and scout all around. But she was thinking of the coming baby. Having a papoose in those caves would be difficult. She knew that she and Nino had to stick together. Having a baby without her sister to help her could be very difficult.

She winced.

'Are you OK?' Nino asked her.

'Sure,' Meralito said. The tone of her voice betrayed her uncertainty.

They groped their way forward among the bats and flickering shadows of the caves. Nino was holding the flaming torch high to see the roof.

'Stop!' Meralito said suddenly.

The two women froze and listened.

'You hear something?' Nino said breathlessly.

'Listen!' Meralito looked back along the passage where they had come.

They both held their breath. For a moment there was silence and then the faint sound of falling rocks and a kind

of slow dragging movement towards them.

'You hear that?' Meralito said in a half whisper. 'There's someone following us.'

They stared at one another, hardly daring to believe what they heard — a steady pulling like someone dragging a sack after them through the dark. Both thought of ancestors and ghosts, visitors from another world, even half human demons. They grabbed each other and shivered.

Meralito was first to get a grip on herself. 'We have to go on,' she whispered. 'Those noises are people. That's Horse Soldier or Jude Riverwind, following us. My guess is Riverwind.'

They moved on cautiously with Jude Riverwind not too far behind, trying to catch up with their light.

* * *

Hawkeye Hank and the boy took the high route which approached the hogan

from above. Charlie was resting as much as possible on his horse's neck. He kept losing consciousness and coming to again. It was hot in the sun and any sensible person would be holed up somewhere waiting for it to cool down. Despite his courage an occasional groan escaped from Charlie's lips, and Hawkeye paused for a while to give him a drink from his canteen.

The boy Manuel scouted ahead. He was nimble and quick as a snake now that he had found Hawkeye and Charlie and he felt a keen responsibility to get them back to the Sweet Spring.

When he had told Hawkeye about the man waiting at the hogan, Hawkeye had nodded and said very little though his eyes had narrowed.

Now Charlie raised his head again. 'What do we aim to do?' he said. His brow was covered with little beads of sweat.

'What we do,' Hawkeye said, 'is we stop right here under this big overhang and you rest up a while in the shade.'

Charlie shook his head and winced. 'I can't do that. If that Horse Soldier is waiting, I want to help.'

Hawkeye reached up to help him down from his horse. 'Best help you can give is if you rest up in the shade.'

'I can shoot,' Charlie protested. 'I lie here thinking about Horse Soldier and our women I'm like to die anyway.'

'You're not going to die,' Hawkeye told him. 'You just rest awhile. Best thing for everybody. You can hold your six shooter in case anyone happens by.'

Charlie rested back on a blanket Hawkeye had laid down for him.

When Hawkeye looked up, he saw Manuel running towards him. 'That *hombre* is still there,' the boy reported. 'Looks like he's sleeping.'

Hawkeye nodded. He had seen killers sleeping before.

'Another thing,' Manuel said in some excitement. 'I saw other men on the trail further down. Can't be sure exactly but I think they might be the men who shot Charlie back in Hopeful.'

Hawkeye narrowed his eyes. 'You see anything of Meralito and Nino?'

The boy shook his head. 'No, like I said, just that man sleeping there and further down the mountain those other *hombres.*'

Hawkeye took his Winchester and made his way to the flat rock that overlooked Sweet Spring. He crawled up to the edge and looked over with Manuel beside him. Though he had no telescope, his eyes were as keen as a hawk's as his name suggested. He saw Horse Soldier sitting there with his Winchester across his knees like a caller waiting but in no hurry to be received. Then he turned to his left where he had a good view of the trail below where Tod Ridelle and the other two were waiting. From that distance he wouldn't have recognized them even if he knew them, and he knew from experience that Horse Soldier couldn't see that part of the trail.

'What do we do?' Manuel whispered.

Hawkeye considered their position.

Horse Soldier and the others were well out of range of his Winchester, anyway. He was thinking specially of Meralito and of the unborn child, and of Nino and Charlie.

He rolled over on his side. 'Listen,' he said. 'You know the caves that run up behind the hogan?'

'I know them,' Manuel affirmed. 'They have many ways.'

'You think you could find your way up there? If I figure right, Meralito and Nino are in those caves somewhere. It's a long way to climb but, if you find them, and tell them about Charlie it would relieve their worries and help some.'

'I find them,' Manuel said eagerly. He was anxious to redeem himself and become a hero.

'Don't take any chances,' Hawkeye said. 'Remember, a trapped snake spits out venom.'

'I remember,' the boy said.

He slithered down from the rock and disappeared like a shadow out of the sun.

★ ★ ★

Horse Soldier wasn't a man to be panicked. He liked to take things one step at a time. So he sat on that stool in front of the hogan and drew out his telescope and scanned the mountains and the rocks all round. It was a barren place yet it had a beauty of its own. There was an awesome silence about it that quietened a man inside. He felt like an insect sitting there under that wide and open sky with the sound of the Sweet Spring plashing close by. Somewhere to the west, rain clouds hovered with a grey screen of rain draped over the earth, somewhere around Hopeful, he thought.

But Horse Soldier had a keen sense of hearing and he listened out for the slightest sound. Sometime Hawkeye Hank would ride in. That's what he figured. Hawkeye Hank must be tired of running. The Colt in Horse Soldier's hand could be mighty persuasive. You give me that stash of gold, we could call

it quits, he thought. It's been a long ride from Texas. Nice for a man to retire at some point in his life. I could sit up here for a hundred years looking across that rugged landscape, he thought.

Then he heard movements, way off somewhere down below. The whinny of a horse. A cloud of dust too. Maybe that's Hawkeye Hank on his way home, he thought.

Anybody watching close might have suspected Horse Soldier was dozing on that stool. He had his black Stetson pulled down so you couldn't see his eyes. The Winchester and the telescope were now beside him on a rock but he had his Colt revolver grasped across his thigh and those eyes were very much alive.

Another slight movement among the rocks? He couldn't be sure. Could be a bird or a snake. But no bird rose and everything became still again except for the flow of the Sweet Spring.

No sound from inside the hogan. That stupid Jude Riverwind might be

having trouble winkling those two women out. In which case you might expect to hear voices arguing in there. It might be wise to go to that curtain again and take a look see.

Horse Soldier stood up and turned towards the hogan just as the Indian Yellow Tail hurled the bowie knife at him. Turning saved Horse Soldier's life. The bowie knife skimmed so close to his ear he felt it like the beat of a bird's wing before it twanged and embedded itself in the side of the hogan.

Horse Soldier turned from the hogan and fired two shots at Yellow Tail. One would have been enough. Yellow Tail was lifted right off his feet. He didn't have time to yell. He just wheeled back and slid like a parcel of waste material down the trail.

Horse Soldier strode to the edge of rock and looked down. Yellow Tail was lying as still as the surrounding rocks. He seemed to be staring up at Horse Soldier in amazement, but he was as dead as a stone.

7

Hawkeye Hank heard those two shots and saw the Indian's body go sliding down the trail. Charlie heard them too. He tried to raise himself and make sure Hawkeye Hank was OK. But he felt so weak he could hardly move and his shoulder was beginning to throb again. Could be I'm going to die after all, he thought in his semi-delirium.

Hawkeye slithered down from the flat rock to check that Charlie was still and quiet and comfortable as possible.

'Are you OK, good buddy?' he said.

'Don't grieve over me,' Charlie croaked. 'You just make sure you and those women are safe.'

Hawkeye crouched down beside Charlie and told him what had happened including the part about sending Manuel up to the cave entrances higher on the mountain.

'You think he has a hell's chance of finding them?' Charlie said pessimistically.

'The boy will do his best,' Hawkeye said. 'And Meralito and Nino know their way around. Another thing, that was Yellow Tail who got shot. Horse Soldier killed him stone dead just like a pesky insect. But Yellow Tail doesn't operate alone. That means those *hombres* who gunned down on you in Hopeful must be moving in.'

He told Charlie he had seen the three riders moving up towards Sweet Spring out of sight of Horse Soldier.

Charlie raised himself on one arm. 'Those men are killers,' he said. 'They mean to get you, claim that reward on your head.'

More like the gold they think I've got, Hawkeye Hank thought.

'Now lie still and quiet in the shade of this rock. Take a drink of water from time to time, and get yourself well.' He brushed a strand of hair away from Charlie's moonlike face and patted his good shoulder.

Charlie forced a smile and sank back again. His experience alone in the hills had taught him patience and courage. He grasped the Colt in his good hand and sank back.

If we don't get help, Charlie's going to die, Hawkeye thought, as he led the horses into a shady hollow close by.

★　★　★

'That sure was a dumb idea,' Handsome Johnny said. 'Sending that stupid Indian up there was a fool thing to do.'

'I told you that Horse Soldier was no man to mess with, didn't I?' Laramie Pete complained lugubriously. 'He's as mean as a skunk and quick as a rattler. Now he'll know we're on our way up to take Hawkeye Hank out, thanks to that skull-brained Indian.'

'Tell you one thing,' Tod Ridelle said. 'Horse Soldier's still setting there like a stuffed bird waiting to be picked off. That's for sure.'

'And who's about to do that?'

Handsome Johnny demanded. 'I get in close enough I could blast him easy.'

'That's my privilege,' Tod Ridelle said. 'I get myself in a good position a little higher up I could drop him with my Winchester. He's setting up there like he's begging to be shot.'

'That would have to be real close and way higher up,' Laramie Pete advised.

'That's no problem to me,' Tod Ridelle said. 'I climb up and get into position up there. I give you a signal with a white bandanna I got. You cover for me. When he returns your fire, I drop him. It's as simple as shelling peas.'

'I've got a better idea,' Laramie Pete said. 'We don't shoot, we talk. Horse Soldier doesn't know who we are and how many we are. When we see that white bandanna we start talking. We do bargaining to take him off guard. We say we're all there for one reason, that's to claim the reward on Hawkeye Hank. We don't mention the gold. Horse Soldier might not know about the gold and he

might not know we know about the gold. While we're talking, you take him out, Tod. How would that be?'

Tod Ridelle thought that might be good enough if he could get close enough and high enough. Laramie Pete was a lugubrious talker, but when he said something it usually made sense.

Handsome Johnny wasn't so impressed. He was still itching for a shoot out with Horse Soldier. 'Better if I climbed up and took a bead on Horse Soldier. I'm a better shot than you, Tod.'

That stung. Tod's face started twitching ferociously. 'You're too eager for blood, Johnny,' he said. 'A man who's eager for blood makes mistakes.'

Handsome Johnny shrugged. 'It's your call with Hawkeye Hank,' he retorted. 'I take out Horse Soldier; you take out Hawkeye Hank. That's a fair deal. Anyway, I can climb up there quicker than you. Stands to reason.'

Laramie Pete grimaced. 'You'll get your chance,' he said to Handsome Johnny. 'There's gonna be plenty of

shooting before this sun sinks. Just as long as I get to doing the bargaining. Horse Soldier knows me. Like I said, we rode together one time.'

Though Handsome Johnny looked none too pleased, that was the end of the argument and Tod Ridelle peeled off with his Winchester and started climbing up to his right where he saw a flat rock from where he might take out Horse Soldier. It was the same flat rock from where Hawkeye Hank and the boy Manuel had watched Horse Soldier.

★   ★   ★

Meralito and Nino had reached a fork in the caves. They stopped to consider their position. In the normal way they could have split up here to confuse their pursuer but Nino knew she couldn't desert Meralito in those circumstances; they had the unborn child to consider. They could still hear the noise that Jude Riverwind was making as he followed them through the cave, and he was

getting much closer.

'What do we do?' Meralito said.

'We go right on,' Nino said. 'Maybe we should put out the torch now we're getting close to the end.'

Dousing the flame was a double blessing. It would take away the light so that Jude Riverwind would have more difficulty in following them, but it would slow them down and Meralito couldn't move fast anyway in her condition.

'We keep going,' Meralito said. 'We're near the end.'

But as they plunged on, the sound of their pursuer's approaching steps got louder. They could hear his laboured breathing. Looking back Nino thought she could see his shadow on the roof of the cave.

Then Jude Riverwind spoke. 'Stop right where you are!' He sounded hoarse and out of breath. 'Stop!' he said again. 'There's nothing to fear. I want to protect you, keep you safe.'

Meralito and Nino looked at one another in astonishment. Could they

believe what they heard?

'You stay back there,' Nino said.

'I come in friendship,' Riverwind protested. He was much closer now, just beyond that last bend in the cave.

'You come in friendship, you stay right where you are,' Meralito cried.

'No need for that, Meralito,' Jude Riverwind replied. 'It's me, Jude River-wind. I don't mean you no harm. I come to offer my protection.'

Now they could see him. He was looking round a ridge in the cave. The light from their torch flickered over his face and gave him a green demonic look. He had a Winchester tucked under his right arm, the barrel pointed towards them.

'What do you want?' Meralito said on the edge of a scream.

'Just wanted to make sure you got to the end of this cave without getting lost,' he said unconvincingly.

'Well, now we got there you don't have anything more to do,' Nino retorted.

Jude Riverwind emerged from behind the ridge and moved towards them with the Winchester raised. 'Now be sensible,' he urged. 'There ain't no need to run from a friend.'

'You say sensible,' Meralito said. 'What's sensible? You led that man up here. He wants Hawkeye's blood. That's your sensible. That's not our sensible.'

Riverwind moved forward another pace and raised the Winchester so that it was pointed straight at Meralito. When he spoke his voice had changed from pleading to threatening. 'Now you move right along and everything's going to be all right,' he said.

Meralito and Nino exchanged looks and moved on towards the cave's exit. Soon they caught a glimmer of welcoming light which got brighter as they moved towards the end of the cave. The three of them emerged from the entrance and blinked around.

'What now?' Meralito asked Riverwind.

'Now we sit and wait,' he said. He wasn't a fast thinker and he needed to figure out his position.

'You've got to let us go,' Nino said. 'My sister Meralito needs to get to our own people. She might need help with the baby.'

Riverwind shook his head. 'I can't do that.' He thought about taking them back through the labyrinth of caves. That way Horse Soldier might give him a bigger cut in that hidden gold. On the other hand, it could be that Meralito knew where that pot of gold lay hidden. 'You know where the gold is?' he asked her.

Meralito and Nino exchanged glances again.

'What gold is that?' Meralito said.

'The gold Hawkeye's got stashed away. My hunch is it must be stashed somewhere in those caves.'

'You're living in some kind of fairyland,' Meralito said with a nervous grin.

Riverwind wasn't impressed. 'You lead me to that gold,' he said, 'then I let

you go free. That's the deal.' He had his left hand on Meralito's shoulder and the Winchester was prodding her side just beside the unborn child.

'You can't do that,' Nino said.

'I think I can,' Riverwind said.

At that moment Meralito made a rash move. From instinct and disgust and the wish to protect the unborn child, she tugged away from Riverwind. Nino took her cue. She grasped the Winchester and pulled it up hard. There was a loud explosion as River-wind involuntarily fired the Winchester.

★　★　★

Charlie had blanked out in the shadow of that big rock. He was dreaming of another spring bigger and deeper than Sweet Spring. He was right under it about to scoop up water and dash it over his face when he woke up shivering and saw the figure of a man creeping up the trail towards him. For a moment he thought it was part of his dream. Then

he came to with a jolt and saw it was Tod Ridelle. Ridelle was carrying a Winchester held loosely at his side. He stopped close by where Charlie lay hidden and looked around. Charlie raised the Colt in his left hand and trained it on Ridelle ready to fire. Normally he could have shot Tod Ridelle right there but he was right-handed and weakened by his wound. So he kept himself still and waited.

He watched as Ridelle looked around warily without seeing him. Ridelle's attention was fixed on the flat rock ahead where Hawkeye and Manuel had climbed up to look down on Horse Soldier. Ridelle would climb up that rock to get a bead on Horse Soldier, but would Horse Soldier be within range of his Winchester? Charlie figured not as he wriggled to one side to get a full view of Ridelle.

Where was Hawkeye? Charlie asked himself. Last time he had seen him he was up on that rock looking down at Horse Soldier. Was he up there still?

Where had he gone? Charlie knew every peak and dip in this rocky landscape and he figured a man would have to be much more than an average shot to wing a person sitting out there beside the Sweet Spring. It was way too far off.

Charlie kept the gun in his hand and rested his head on a stone. OK, he thought, so what happens now?

★ ★ ★

When Tod Ridelle reached the top of the flat rock and looked down on Sweet Spring he knew he hadn't a hope of a snowflake in hell of winging Horse Soldier from up there. He looked over the edge of the rock and saw Handsome Johnny and Laramie Pete edging their way forward under cover towards Horse Soldier who still appeared to be dozing in front of the hogan.

He thought, maybe I couldn't gun down on Horse Soldier from here with any accuracy but, if I aim high enough I

might bring one down so close it might distract his attention long enough for Johnny and Pete to get a shot at him. It could be that's the best way.

Then he said, 'What the hell! I'm not here to get Horse Soldier. I'm here to get Hawkeye Hank!'

He swung towards where Handsome Johnny and Laramie Pete had been but they were no longer there. They must have been getting themselves into a better position for an attack on Horse Soldier.

What should he do? Maybe he should climb down and work his way further on to get a better shot. But he didn't get a chance to decide. Before he could make a decision he heard Laramie Pete's voice echoing on the mountainside. Pete had a deep and powerful baritone and he might have been great singing in a choir or something 'civilized'.

'Hi there, Horse Soldier!' he boomed out. 'You up there? I can see you real good from here.'

What a dumb thing to do! Tod

173

Ridelle thought. He hadn't given a signal with his white bandanna and he wasn't within range for a good shot. So, what could he do? He'd have to take a chance. He levered his Winchester and wriggled himself into a good position for the best shot. Hold your fire, he thought. Wait for the right moment and listen and watch.

He could see Horse Soldier, sitting in front of the hogan with his six-shooter in his hand, but Horse Soldier gave no sign he had heard Laramie Pete's voice.

Then that voice came echoing round again. 'Remember me, Horse Soldier? Laramie Pete. We rode together once or twice. One time we were buddies. remember that?'

Horse Soldier raised his head a little but gave no other sign.

'Can you hear me?' Laramie Pete boomed out again. 'You know what, we're here for the same thing, Horse. Why don't we do a deal. You want the gold. We want the gold. You want the reward; we want the reward. Why don't

we do a deal together?'

Horse Soldier shifted his head a little but said nothing.

Laramie Pete might have been getting a little frustrated, Tod Ridelle thought, but Laramie Pete pressed on. 'Tell you something,' he said. 'I worked out where that gold is hid. Why don't we do a trade off? We work together, share out the gold. How would that be?'

What would Horse Soldier say about that? Tod Ridelle wondered. Now Horse Soldier moved. He holstered his Colt, picked up his Winchester and levered it. Then he spoke. 'That's no deal, Pete. And I do remember you. I remember you as a sidewinding, treacherous, ugly skunk. That's what I remember. How will that do for a start?'

There was a momentary pause as Laramie Pete considered the situation or possibly to let Handsome Johnny creep up into a better position. Then he spoke again.

'That was a long time back.' He gave a low gravelly laugh. 'And you're

thinking of the wrong man. Why don't we get wise together? We could all be richer before the sun sets on this day.'

Tod Ridelle hesitated no longer. He pushed his Winchester up to get the best trajectory so the bullet might drop down as close to Horse Soldier's head as possible. Everything that goes up must come down. It would be a chancy shot but it might just work if he kept himself steady. But before he could squeeze the trigger, something unexpected happened: Horse Soldier disappeared!

★   ★   ★

Nino and Jude Riverwind were wrestling over the Winchester. When the Winchester had discharged itself Nino had felt something like a fire raging close to her ear. Now it was giving her excruciating pain as though someone was gouging out her ear. Not enough to weaken her but enough to raise her fury. Nino was a slim, quiet woman but she had a deal of grit, specially when

she was roused.

They wrestled backwards and forwards to get possession of the Winchester. Meralito was trying to intervene but the two struggling figures moved backwards and forwards so fast she couldn't make a grab at either of them. Then Nino used her knee to jab Jude Riverwind in the groin. If you're going to knee a man in the groin you have to do it hard enough to double him up and put him on the ground. Otherwise he becomes like a raging bull and that's what happened to Riverwind. He half fell against a rock and then rose with a roar of anger and came at a rush towards Nino. Nino had the Winchester in her hand and she tried to swing it towards Riverwind and cover him, but, before she could lever it, Riverwind was on her again. He wrenched the Winchester violently from her hand and turned it on her.

'Stay where you are!' he said breathlessly. 'You come any closer, I kill you.' He looked as though he meant it, too. He swung the Winchester towards

Meralito. 'You, too. I kill you, too.' He had his back to the mountainside. He was gulping to get his breath, but he looked like he meant business.

'Don't you understand?' Nino shouted. 'Meralito's going to have her baby. I got to look after her!'

Riverwind was grinning. 'I don't give a damn about Meralito's baby. That's Hawkeye's baby too. I don't give a shit about Hawkeye Hank. He's gonna get what's coming to him. That's what's gonna happen to Hawkeye.'

As he spoke Meralito gasped and doubled up, clutching her belly.

Jude laughed and pulled down the lever of the Winchester. Was he about to shoot? They never found out. At that moment something surprising intervened. There was a dull thud and something struck Riverwind right between the eyes. His head jerked back, a look of astonishment appeared on his face, he dropped the Winchester and sank forward onto his knees. The next second, before either of the women could move, Riverwind

collapsed forward and had a shuddering fit.

The boy Manuel sprang down from the rock where he had been crouching and ran forward. He placed his foot on Riverwind's chest and looked down into his glazed eyes. It was like David looking down at the defeated Goliath.

'I think I killed him,' he said in astonishment.

Nino came forward, grabbed the Winchester, and trained it on Riverwind's inert body. 'I think you did,' she said.

* * *

Horse Soldier had vanished. He was a fast mover. Tod Ridelle couldn't figure whether he had disappeared into the hogan or gone someplace else. That was a deceptive, rock-strewn place. He had disappeared in less than a second. While Ridelle was working the lever of his Winchester and getting himself into a good position for a shot, Horse

Soldier had moved with the speed of light.

Like Pete said, he thought, there's no messing with Horse Soldier. A shadow seemed to fall across the sun and he looked up to see a man dressed like a Navajo with a headband and a long smock looking down at him.

'You looking for someone?' Hawkeye Hank said. Tod Ridelle's eye started to twitch overtime. The man looking down at him had brick-red cheeks and a beard and he had a glint of steel in his eyes. He also had a Winchester trained on him.

Tod tried to think what to do. Lying there he was at a considerable disadvantage.

'If you're thinking of shooting someone down there, I think you're fooling yourself,' Hawkeye Hank said. 'Got the wrong man too.' He grinned through his beard. 'That Horse Soldier never did you any harm, now, did he?'

Tod Ridelle made no reply.

'Now why don't you relieve yourself

of that useless fire-stick before it goes off and does somebody harm?' Hawkeye Hank said. 'That way we might come to some understanding.'

Tod Ridelle's face was twitching overtime. He was reluctant to let go of the Winchester, but it seemed the only sensible thing to do. So he laid it on the rock and slid it towards Hawkeye Hank.

Hawkeye Hank gathered it in with his foot and shoved it over the edge of the rock. And in that split second Tod Ridelle saw his chance. He reached for Hawkeye Hank's leg and jerked it towards him. Hawkeye Hank reeled back, overbalanced, and fell.

* * *

Laramie Pete and Handsome Johnny were staring at one another in disbelief. Where had that dozing *hombre* gone?

'That's what I warned you,' Laramie Pete said. 'There's no messing with Horse Soldier. You think he's asleep, he's just waiting to strike.'

'What do we do now?' Handsome Johnny said. You could tell by his voice he was no longer quite so cocksure. He looked all round, keeping his head as low as possible in case Horse Soldier was hiding close waiting to take a shot at him.

Laramie Pete was trying to make a practical assessment. Horse Soldier might have been in the hogan or in the barn. How could he have moved so quickly? It made you feel creepy in your spine. Horse Soldier seemed to know what a man was thinking before he knew himself.

'Tell you one thing,' he said. 'I figure we're in a bad position here. Be good to make a tactical withdrawal.'

'What does that mean?' Handsome Johnny said.

'That means we go back to the horses and wait on Tod. This is his call. He has to decide on the next move.'

Johnny shook his head. 'I don't think so,' he said. 'Anyway, you spoke out before he waved his white bandanna.

Maybe we should have waited.'

'Waited hell!' Laramie Pete said. 'Look what's happening anyway.' He pointed up at the rocks above on their right. What they saw was two men bashing daylights out of one another up there. First they saw what looked like Tod Ridelle hammering away. Then he disappeared and they saw another figure punching away equally hard. It was like a distant puppet show with silhouettes.

'Who the hell is that?' Handsome Johnny marvelled.

'Whoever it is, it don't look good,' Laramie Pete said.

★ ★ ★

Tod Ridelle was no mean fist fighter. Years ago he had taken lessons and done some bare-knuckle fighting in the ring. You never know when you might have to use your fists to get out of a tight corner. He smashed his right fist against Hawkeye's jaw and Hawkeye staggered back against the edge of the flat

rock. Another inch and he would topple over and plunge to his death. That's a mean way to go, Hawkeye thought as he shook his head clear. Tod Ridelle was dancing around like a professional pugilist looking for a knock out blow. Now his face had stopped twitching and he looked as mean as a starving mountain bear.

'Say your prayers, Hawkeye!' he shouted. 'I'm coming in to take that reward. Dead or alive it says and I don't give a damn either way.'

He took a wild swing at Hawkeye and his fist went wide. Hawkeye went down on one knee and caught his breath. A cascade of thoughts careered through his brain: Charlie lying there injured in the cave below; Horse Soldier sitting there somewhere waiting to shoot him down; Meralito and Nino and the unborn baby. It was the last thought that spurred him back to life. As Tod Ridelle swung his fist again, Hawkeye ducked low and launched forward with a head butt into Ridelle's midriff.

Ridelle staggered back with a grunt and sprawled out on the rock.

Then there was a brief pause in the battle as each man struggled to his feet and laboured to get his breath back. They both rose in the same moment. They were circling each other like snarling wolves. Hawkeye was spitting out blood and fragments of tooth. Tod Ridelle had his left hand pressed to his gut. He breathed hard for moment.

'You killed my brother,' he snarled. 'I'm gonna make you pay for that, you pretend Navajo Injun.'

Hawkeye said nothing. He figured he didn't have enough breath to waste.

'OK,' Tod Ridelle growled. 'You know what you do? You just come real quiet before I grind your face to powder on this flat rock and split your skull or I'm gonna splash your whole rotten carcass on those rocks below. You hear me?'

'I hear you,' Hawkeye said from his broken mouth.

'OK, that's what it's gonna be!' Tod

Ridelle waded in for the kill.

Hawkeye Hank smelt the bitter stink of defeat in his nostrils. But he had a lot riding on him. As Tod Ridelle came in hard and confident, he sent a rain of sharp blows against his body and his head. The last blow crashed against Ridelle's nose and squashed it flat with a sound like a ripe fruit caught under the rim of a wagon wheel.

Ridelle staggered back and clutched what was left of his nose. Hawkeye was no professional but he sure packed a punch! Ridelle's hand came away bleeding and he was gasping and spitting out bits of tooth and gum and snorting streams of blood from his pulpy nose.

Then he made a big mistake. He looked round quickly for the remaining Winchester, probably thinking he could swing it at Hawkeye and break his leg. But Hawkeye had kicked that Winchester right over the edge of the rock.

Now Ridelle saw the black pit of

defeat opening under him. But a defeated man doesn't become calm. He's just like a rabid dog, blind with fury. Ridelle forgot all the pugilistic skills he had learned. He just came roaring in like the wild tornado that beats down everything before it.

Hawkeye was still panting but his brain was clear. Everything happened in slow motion. Instead of crashing against the body of flesh intent on pulverizing him, he caught at the man's sleeve and helped him along, turning by instinct and helping him in the direction he was headed. Tod Ridelle crashed against the edge of that great slab of rock and stood there flailing with his arms. He must have seen the jagged rocks below rushing up to meet him as he plunged to his death.

8

'My gawd, you see that?' Laramie Pete exclaimed. 'That was Ridelle plunging down the cliff there.'

There was no need to explain. Anybody could have heard Ridelle's scream as he hurtled towards those needle-sharp rocks below.

But when Laramie Pete turned to look at Handsome Johnny, Johnny was nowhere to be seen. Yes, he had heard the scream and watched Ridelle's body cartwheeling towards its doom. But Handsome Johnny's blood lust was not diminished. That damned fool, he said to himself. He should have stayed down here and concentrated on the business. Now Johnny was intent on getting closer to the Sweet Spring. Yes, Horse Soldier was quick and good and deadly with a gun according to reputation, but he was also human and people have feet

of clay. Someone had to take Horse Soldier and Hawkeye Hank out and that someone would be him. Laramie wants to chicken out, that's OK by me. I claim the reward and get that big fat stash of gold. Watch your back, Horse Soldier, I'm coming to get you!

Now he was out of Laramie Pete's sight. He was slithering up among the rocks like a lizard or a snake with its poisonous fangs ready to strike. Soon he would reach the hogan and Horse Soldier must show himself. And that would be Handsome Johnny's chance. He had a fleeting vision of fulfilling his mission, killing Horse Soldier and spending all those dollars and all that gold in those honky tonks some place. But he also had a crafty plan in the back of his mind too and that could wait on the future.

★　★　★

Horse Soldier was watching from his place of concealment right by the

189

cascade. He was standing in the shadows so close to the falling water that only a trained observer could have seen him. It was a little splashy and wet in that half hidden place but Horse Soldier kept himself as still as the rock of ages. He too had seen the falling body but he hadn't heard the scream because of the cascading water. He had his telescope trained on the flat rock. and he watched as Hawkeye Hank stood panting above, looking down at the impaled figure of the dead man below.

That's Hawkeye Hank, he thought. That's the *hombre* I'm here to get, dead or alive. He had to admire the way Hawkeye Hank had fought with his opponent and thrown him down on to those rocks.

Apart from the movement of the telescope Horse Soldier kept himself still and wondered how many more men he had to kill before he could claim his reward. He could see the body of Yellow Tail lying on the trail below

but those two sightless staring eyes didn't trouble him. A stiff is a stiff anyway you look at it. Let the dead look after themselves and concentrate your mind on the living. Matter of honour and respect and common savvy too!

His thoughts turned to the two women and on Jude Riverwind and he chuckled quietly to himself. He knew Riverwind hadn't a hope in hell of tracking those women in their own caves, or come to that of finding his way out again.

The big disadvantage for Horse Soldier was being concealed beside that waterfall and not being able to hear what was going on around you. A man might creep up on you and drop you before you had time to react. That's if he saw you before you saw him. He figured there were two ornery fools trying to creep in and gun him down.

★   ★   ★

Laramie Pete was a pragmatist. That is, he weighed things up and never took

unnecessary chances. OK, let Handsome Johnny do what he had to do. If he got Horse Soldier, what the hell! Horse Soldier wasn't Hawkeye Hank and Hawkeye Hank was the prize. Laramie Pete knew where Hawkeye Hank was. If Pete bided his time, he might get rich after all. If there was gold hidden somewhere, he had as much right to it as any other man — more, maybe, since he had brains and knew how to use them. That's what he figured, anyway, as he crouched among the rocks not too far below the level area where the hogan stood. Handsome Johnny might kill Horse Soldier; it was a remote possibility but with a man like Horse Soldier you had to show respect. You didn't respect Horse Soldier you ended up dead.

Then to his surprise he heard Handsome Johnny's voice and it was coming from a little to his left, much closer to the hogan than he would have expected.

'Hi there, Horse Soldier!' Handsome

Johnny crowed out. 'I come to do you a deal. Like Pete said, we come in peace. We figure we all want the same thing. Three guns are better than one. That's a matter of common savvy.'

Laramie Pete raised his head a little and saw to his surprise a slight movement close to the Sweet Spring. Could it be that that strutting peacock had lured Horse Soldier out of his place of concealment? Laramie Pete edged forward a little and raised his Winchester. Keep talking, Johnny, he thought. He kills you, I might kill him. Things were beginning to look brighter in Laramie Pete's world.

Then he heard Horse Soldier speak and saw him more clearly as he moved away from the Sweet Spring.

'What's your idea of the deal?' Horse Soldier demanded.

Handsome Johnny came back, 'Like I said, we both want the same thing,' he crowed again.

You show yourself, you get yourself a mouthful of lead, Laramie Pete thought.

Horse Soldier was almost in his sights but not quite. Pete would need to get into a better, more level, position to bring Horse Soldier down. So he edged up a bit more and sent a small shower of rocks tumbling away. Not much, but Horse Soldier had a keen sense of hearing even under that waterfall. Laramie Pete ducked down as Horse Soldier's eyes came round to locate him.

'What had you in mind?' Horse Soldier said.

'Well,' Handsome Johnny said, 'I guess we should talk a little, come to some kind of agreement.'

'OK, then, come here and talk,' Horse Soldier challenged in a somewhat jeering tone.

There was an ominous pause. He's giving me the break I need, Pete thought. As soon as Horse Soldier comes out to meet Johnny, I can get a bead on him and bring him down.

Then Johnny made his big mistake. Was it foolhardiness or courage? 'I'm on my way,' he said.

Horse Soldier turned and Pete saw Handsome Johnny move up onto the level place where the hogan stood. Horse Soldier and Handsome Johnny were facing each other no more ten paces apart. Both were holding Winchesters but neither seemed too eager to use them.

'So now I see you,' Horse Soldier said.

'Now you see me,' Handsome Johnny agreed.

'You want to make a suggestion?' Horse Soldier asked.

'We could start by laying down our Winchesters,' said Handsome Johnny. 'That way we could talk more free.'

'That sounds like a reasonable idea,' Horse Soldier said. He drew his Winchester across his body and trailed it loose in his left hand. 'Your turn now,' he said.

Handsome Johnny seemed to shrug. He bent his knees and laid his Winchester on the ground. Each man now had a handgun in a holster by his side.

This was almost mesmerizing to Laramie Pete who raised his head to see better. Then he steadied his Winchester against a rock and tried to bring Horse Soldier into his sights.

'Now you wanna talk?' Horse Soldier said.

'Sure I wanna talk.' Handsome Johnny was crouching. Pete could read his thoughts. Handsome Johnny took pride in that position and he thought he could beat any man on earth to the draw. He would draw and palm-fan his shooter as quickly as a rattler shooting its venom.

Laramie Pete took a deep breath and eased the trigger finger on his Winchester. This was his chance to bring down Horse Soldier.

The next instant everything seemed to happen in slow motion, just like they say in the books. Horse Soldier did a kind of stooping motion and came up with his hogleg blazing. Handsome Johnny discharged his weapon not more than a tenth of a second later, but that

tenth of a second was fatal. Johnny leaped back from his crouching position and seemed to hang in the smoky air for a second before plunging onto his back. He raised his head as if he wanted to say a word to Horse Soldier. Blood spurted from between his lips and he fell back dead as a post.

A second later, Laramie Pete fired his Winchester and felt it buck against his shoulder. Horse Soldier spun round in his direction with his Colt revolver in his hand.

★   ★   ★

The boy Manuel was staring at the face of the man he had killed. Then he took him by the feet and dragged him, bumping arms sprawled out, away from the two women. Jude Riverwind was no lightweight and it took a deal of tugging.

'Leave him!' Nino said. 'There's nothing you can do for him now.'

Manuel hesitated. He was in a state

of shock. He had never killed a man before, never intended to. Then he knew what he had to do. 'I got to get back to Charlie and Hawkeye, tell them you're safe.'

Nino didn't know about that. Meralito was so close to her time it might be better to do something more practical.

'Charlie needs me,' Manuel asserted. 'Charlie and Hawkeye need to know you're OK.' He stooped and grabbed the flaming torch and the Winchester.

'What do you aim to do?' Nino asked in desperation.

'I'm going back through the cave,' Manuel said illogically.

'You can't do that!' Meralito said. 'That man Horse Soldier is at the other end of the caves. He'll be waiting. Anyway, you might get lost in there.' Then she winced and grasped her abdomen.

'I won't get lost,' the boy boasted. 'I know my way blind in there.'

'You take care now,' Nino said

fearfully. She knew Manuel well: he was a wild headstrong kid and you couldn't change his mind once he was set on something.

'You take care now,' Meralito echoed.

The boy shrugged and ventured into the cave. Riding with Charlie and learning to be a man had given him courage. It was very dark and gloomy in there, but he knew the way. He raised the torch up high and moved cautiously but boldly into the labyrinth. That boy had enough sand in his craw for two men!

★ ★ ★

When Hawkeye Hank heard the shots he was bending over Charlie soothing away the sweat from his forehead. Charlie had a slight fever which was not a good sign. I've got to get Charlie into the hogan and get some kind of medical help, he thought. 'You think you could get back on your horse when it gets cooler?' he said.

Charlie raised his head and gave a doleful smile. 'Sure,' he said. 'Just as soon as I can stretch out, I'll be OK.' He closed his eyes and opened them again. 'Did I dream it, or did I hear shooting?'

'You heard shooting,' Hawkeye told him. 'But that's no nevermind, it doesn't concern you.'

'Just as long as Nino and Meralito are OK,' Charlie said.

'They're OK. No harm will come to them,' Hawkeye reassured him. But Hawkeye did not feel reassured. He was thinking of Meralito and the unborn child. That was his main concern.

★　★　★

Laramie Pete cursed his luck. As he fired his Winchester, Horse Soldier moved to one side. It was only a fraction of an inch but enough for the shot to go wide. Could be the shock of seeing Handsome Johnny falling dead had something to do with it but there

was no time to think about that. Horse Soldier had loosed one off at him and it too had missed. Laramie Pete was not a man to panic. He lived by his own code, and knew that anyone who lost control was likely to lose his life as well.

As soon as Horse Soldier had fired his first shot at Laramie Pete he had ducked and disappeared as quick as a mountain lion. The shot had whined an inch past Pete's ear and Pete knew he was in trouble. So he drew back and slithered away. As he knew from experience, you had to have a lot of know-how to avoid a Horse Soldier bullet. Horse Soldier moved like a cat through long grass. You never knew which way he would strike.

Laramie Pete quietened his breath and listened. Keep as quiet as a mouse and still your breathing, he advised himself. He even closed his eyes momentarily to listen and concentrate.

Then he *did* hear a sound. It was faint, no more than a slither, a sliding among the rocks, but it was a sign. He

levered his Winchester and swung round ready to fire, but, even as he moved, he knew he was a fraction of a second too late. Horse Soldier came looming towards him. Though he lurched sideways and almost lost his footing, he took a quick shot with his Colt and rock fragments sprayed up a whisker away from Pete's head.

Pete fired a quick shot from his Winchester but Horse Soldier had slithered sideways out of sight.

'Hold your fire!' Laramie Pete shouted. 'We don't need to do this!' But deep in his heart he knew it was too late. You can't bargain with a man like Horse Soldier when he has the iron in his soul.

Horse Soldier was laughing close by like he was enjoying the experience. 'You don't hold your fire, Pete. It's you or me and I figure it's gonna be you.'

Pete fired another round in the direction of the voice and levered the Winchester again. But that was a false move. You don't make that kind of error with a man like Horse Soldier. Horse

Soldier stood right up like he was daring Laramie to fire at him again, but Laramie Pete never got in that second shot because Horse Soldier fired two shots. The first ripped through Pete's shoulder, spinning him round like a top, the second struck him plumb in the middle of his forehead. Pete jerked back and slithered away among the rocks.

Horse Soldier walked down and looked into his dead eyes.

'Too bad,' he said. 'Too bad, you damned fool!'

★ ★ ★

The boy Manuel heard the shots from inside the cave but he moved on stealthily with the flaming torch held high and the Winchester trailed in his left hand. He wasn't sure what he had to do but he knew he had to do something for Charlie and Hawkeye's sake. For Meralito and Nino's sakes too. When he reached almost to the end

of the tunnel where it opened into the hogan, he extinguished the torch and laid it on the floor of the cave. Then he levered the Winchester so that he had a slug engaged, pulled aside the buffalo skin and stepped cautiously into the hogan.

All seemed to be still. There was nobody at home.

He crept stealthily into the room where the lamp was still burning low. Everything seemed strangely quiet and peaceful as though the whole place was holding its breath and waiting for something to happen. Manuel moved across to the entrance and cautiously pulled the buffalo skin curtain aside.

No one.

He went out on to the terrace where Meralito spread her woven blankets and saw that the fire was still smouldering as though inviting visitors to sit down and share a pipe or a drink. He held the Winchester out in front of him and then saw the dead man lying face up with blood on his mouth. For a

moment he thought he saw the body twitch and move. Then he heard a faint sound behind him and he turned.

Horse Soldier was standing a couple of paces away. He had his Stetson pulled down over his eyes and to Manuel he looked like an incarnation of the Devil himself.

Manuel froze and felt himself go numb all over.

'Who are you?' he said.

Horse Soldier shook his head slowly and said, 'I might ask you the same question.'

'Manuel,' the boy said. Talking to the Devil was kind of hard. 'I heard shooting.'

'Necessary hazard of the trade,' Horse Soldier said.

Manuel was holding the Winchester as though ready to fire it if needed. 'You're Horse Soldier,' he said. 'You killed this man who shot Charlie.' He gestured towards the body of Handsome Johnny.

Horse Soldier nodded. 'Self defence. He tried to kill me.'

'This is Hawkeye Hank's place, him and Meralito,' the boy said.

'That's right,' Horse Soldier replied. 'That's why I'm here visiting.'

Manuel wasn't satisfied. He had killed one man to protect Meralito and Nino. He felt he had the drop on Horse Soldier. Horse Soldier had laid his Winchester down. Now all he had was the Colt revolver which had killed Handsome Johnny. Manuel felt brave, exhilarated, perhaps.

Horse Soldier seemed to be laughing. 'Why don't you stop waving that thing about. You're making me dizzy,' he said.

Manuel steadied the Winchester and held it still in Horse Soldier's direction. 'I know you,' he said. 'You're a bounty hunter and you've come to take Hawkeye in and I'm not going to let that happen.'

Horse Soldier narrowed his eyes and swayed forward. 'I hope you can use that thing.'

'I can use it,' Manuel said. 'If I have to use it to stop you killing Hawkeye, I will.'

Horse Soldier swayed slightly again. 'Listen, kid,' he said. 'I aim to say this once and only once. I don't kill children and I don't kill women. That's not part of my game.'

Manuel held himself up. His knees were trembling but he didn't want to show his fear. He had to protect Hawkeye and Charlie and those two women. 'You want to take Hawkeye in you're going to have to kill me,' he said. He raised the Winchester up to his shoulder and aimed it just below Horse Soldier's black Stetson.

Horse Soldier was as still as the statue of a man. He held his right hand above the butt of the Colt, but he didn't draw.

Then came another sound, the sound of approaching hoofs. Manuel looked beyond the bounty hunter and saw two horsemen come along the trail. One was Hawkeye Hank and the other, riding low in the saddle, was Charlie Silversmith.

9

Hawkeye Hank knew well what he was doing as he rode past the inert body of Yellow Tail. It was still shy of sunset and the rocks were radiating heat, but the air was a tad cooler. Charlie had complained but Hawkeye had insisted, so they rode on quietly but resolutely towards the hogan that was Hawkeye's home.

As they drew close Hawkeye saw the boy Manuel standing legs braced with the Winchester pointed directly at Horse Soldier's head. Though Horse Soldier had heard the sound of the horses, he didn't turn completely. Hawkeye figured he had started to take the boy seriously. Hawkeye Hank knew Manuel was a loyal boy and that he would do anything to save his friend and mentor Charlie. Hawkeye Hank figured enough blood had been shed.

So he drew rein and held up his hand.

'No more shooting,' he said. 'Manuel put up your gun.'

Manuel glanced at the two riders and Charlie raised his head. 'Do as the man says,' he croaked.

Hawkeye Hank knew he was taking a chance. In that split second Horse Soldier could draw his Colt and fire. He might kill Manuel, and shoot Charlie and him down from their horses. But Hawkeye Hank thought it was a chance worth taking and he figured correctly.

Manuel lowered the Winchester and Horse Soldier turned slowly towards them.

'I'm coming in,' Hawkeye said. 'Bringing my friend Charlie Silversmith. He's wounded bad and needs to lie down and get back his strength.'

Horse Soldier's eye went to Charlie and he nodded.

'Ease down, buddy,' Hawkeye Hank said to Charlie when they had got up close to the hogan. Charlie tried not to groan as Hawkeye eased him down

from the horse's back.

Horse Soldier made no move to assist. He stood and watched as Hawkeye and Manuel helped Charlie into the hogan. After a few minutes Hawkeye Hank and Manuel emerged from the hogan.

'Go look after the horses,' Hawkeye said to the boy, and Manuel led the horses away to the barn for feed and rest.

★　★　★

Hawkeye Hank turned to Horse Soldier who nodded as though things were turning out much as he had expected.

'Well, I'm here,' Hawkeye Hank said.

Horse Soldier replied, 'I've been waiting on you. Knew you'd show up sooner or later.'

'Could have been later,' Hawkeye said. ''Cept that my buddy needs to be lying down in the cool.'

Horse Soldier nodded. 'Looks like he'll recover with the right treatment.'

'That's my hope,' Hawkeye confirmed.

Horse Soldier was grinning under his Stetson. 'Saw you throw that *hombre* down from that high bluff. Where did you learn to do that?'

'You don't learn it, it comes by instinct. A man thinks he's about to die, nature tells him what to do.'

Horse Soldier was still grinning. 'It didn't tell those other *hombres* much, did it? That one lying dead over there thought he could beat me to the draw. That was cocksure. A man who is cocksure never wins.' He nodded in the direction of the rocky scrub below. 'And that other one with a face like a twisted pine. He wasn't cocksure. He just lost confidence when he saw the other one die.' He raised his hand fatalistically. 'That's the way it happens sometimes.'

A philosopher, Hawkeye thought. This man's a thinker.

'Why don't we sit down here for a while?' he said.

'Sure.' Horse Soldier sat down on a

stool and watched the light fading behind the rocky silhouette. Soon the coyotes would be howling among the rocks. Before that it would be decision time.

'Manuel tells me you were good to Meralito and Nino,' Hawkeye Hank remarked.

Horse Soldier raised his head. 'I don't harm women. Matter of honour. Women and children. Code of the profession, you understand.' He paused. 'I noticed, by the way, one of them was far gone with child.'

'That's Meralito. She carrying my child.' Hawkeye Hank was beginning to wonder why he was being so companionable with this man. Horse Soldier seemed to relax. Hawkeye thought he might produce a pipe at any moment, load it with tobacco, and sit there smoking. Instead, Horse Soldier produced a small flask of whiskey. He took a swig and handed it to Hawkeye. Hawkeye raised his hand in refusal. 'Suit yourself.' Horse Soldier took back the flask.

The two men sat contemplating the sinking sun for a minute or two.

'What's the deal?' Hawkeye asked.

Horse Soldier considered for a while. 'Maybe we should bury those bodies. They'll be starting to stink. And those coyotes howling out there will be sneaking in to tear them to pieces. Not a purty sight. You kill a man you owe him a good burial whatever you think of him. Matter of honour.'

Hawkeye Hank regarded him steadily for a moment and decided he wasn't joking.

'You know somewhere close by with soil loose enough to dig?' Horse Soldier asked.

'Only my wife's vegetable patch. Don't want them there. Don't want those bodies close to the place,' Hawkeye said. 'Better off in Boot Hill, Little Butte.'

'Guess we could arrange that,' Horse Soldier said. 'We round up their horses and take them down come morning.'

He took another swig.

Horse Soldier was like a poker player, a master of bluff and finesse. You couldn't tell which way he would jump and which cards he had hidden under the table. One thing was sure: he intended to stick around even after the sun had gone down behind the mountain.

★　★　★

Charlie was feeling a whole lot better lying in the shade inside the hogan. It had the smell of home about it. He had sat there many times with Meralito and Nino and Hawkeye, and, if he had to die, this might be the best place. But right now he began to feel he might not die after all.

Manuel his attendant was fussing round him like an old granny woman.

'What's happening out there?' Charlie asked the boy.

Manuel peeped out through the buffalo hide curtain. 'Hawkeye and that Horse Soldier are setting together.

214

Horse Soldier is drinking and Hawkeye is just looking.'

Charlie was up on one elbow. I might have to take things into my own hands and kill that bounty hunter, he thought, but there were other things on his mind too. 'Tell me what happened to Nino and Meralito,' he said.

Manuel told him how he had killed Jude Riverwind and dragged him away and how Meralito and Nino had asked him to go and reassure the men and that Meralito was very close to her time.

'Listen,' Charlie said, leaning towards him. 'You did a brave but foolish thing out there with Horse Soldier. He could have killed you stone dead before you could squeeze the trigger. You hear me?'

'I hear you,' Manuel felt proud and ashamed at the same time.

Charlie reached for the boy's hand. 'You did good,' he said. 'Now I want for you to go out along that dark cave and find those two womenfolk. Can you do that?'

'Sure I can,' the boy said with reviving spirits. 'I know the way through there without a light.'

'OK,' Charlie said. 'Now you take the Winchester and go.'

'What about you?' Manuel said.

'Don't worry about me. I'm going to be OK, and I might be a lot more useful here. Just look out for those two womenfolk.' He squeezed the boy's hand. 'Now go.'

Manuel took a quick look out onto the terrace and saw that Hawkeye and Horse Soldier were still sitting murmuring quietly together. Manuel shook his head. He couldn't figure out exactly what was going on.

Charlie gestured with his hand at Manuel and the boy slipped out between the back curtain and disappeared into the darkness.

*   *   *

Sheriff Wills had heard the shooting when he was quite far back on the trail.

Was he relieved or apprehensive? He couldn't make up his mind. He just knew he was riding up to Sweet Spring to prevent murder and mayhem and maybe it was already too late. The sun was low on the mountain and it would be time to call it a day. So he looked for a place to tether his horse and lay his bedroll down. It wasn't easy in this rough and rocky land and, like his wife kept reminding him, Wills was no longer a young man.

As he considered the matter he heard the whinny of horses and his own horse responded. Sheriff Wills knew about horses. As a young man he had served on a ranch and he knew horse language and he guessed those horses were restless and anxious. So he rode on a little more cautiously and found them in a little gully with a trickle of water close by the trail, three horses and a mule. Wills dismounted, made soothing noises and ran his hands over the flanks of the horses to calm them

down. Then he recognized the mule from its particular markings and the star on its forehead.

'You must be Yellow Tail's mule,' he said quietly to the agitated mule. 'That means Yellow Tail is around here some place.'

That was bad medicine. It confirmed his worst fears. He knew that those who wanted to kill Hawkeye Hank had got there before him.

'No use to fret,' he said to himself philosophically. 'Better to just hunker down and wait till sunup.'

There was a little creek spouting up between the rocks: a good place to rest. So he led his horse to the creek and let it drink. There was rough and withered grass around too, so this was the place to put down his temporary roots.

Sheriff Wills lit a small fire, opened a can of beans and sat back with the relative comfort of his pipe. 'Come sunup, I'll ride on to the Sweet Spring and see what needs to be done,' he said to himself.

'Where's the boy?' Hawkeye Hank asked from the entrance to the hogan.

'The boy's good. I sent him out to locate Nino and Meralito,' Charlie said.

Hawkeye Hank said, 'He did a damned fool thing out there. You confront a man like Horse Soldier you're liable to end up dead.'

Hawkeye Hank adjusted the reed lamp and the interior of the hogan shone up bright and clear. It was now almost dark outside. Hawkeye knew about the death of Jude Riverwind but he was worried about Meralito and his unborn child. 'I could go out through the cave myself,' he said.

'Where is Horse Soldier?' Charlie asked.

Hawkeye shook his head. 'I don't rightly know,' he said. 'We talked for a while and he offered me a drink. Then he took his horse out of the barn and made off somewhere.'

'Without saying anything?' Charlie asked.

Hawkeye stood there turning things over in his mind. 'Those two women must be right hungry,' he said. 'Meralito needs to keep her strength up for the baby's sake and for her own sake too.'

'They probably made towards the canyon. That's where our people like to have their babies.'

That was true, Hawkeye thought. He knew that Nino was a very responsible young woman. So she would know what to do. But he was still worried.

'You say Horse Soldier just lit out without saying a word,' Charlie said.

'He just said, 'See you come sunup',' Hawkeye said. 'Casual like just as though everything was arranged between us. I was going quietly according to him. That's what I figure his plan is anyway.'

Charlie raised his head a little. 'I don't get this. Why don't you go out through the caves?' he suggested. 'That Horse Soldier comes back in the morning, he'll find you gone. He'll just find a Navajo man lying here pointing a

Colt revolver at him.'

Hawkeye grinned. 'I can't do that, Charlie. I have a hunch Horse Soldier would shoot you dead, no matter you're wounded.' He sucked his teeth. 'Another thing. If I went out through that back way, Horse Soldier would follow to the ends of the wide world. You think he hasn't figured I might try to get away? He might even hope for it. Horse Soldier likes to think he's a man who never gives up. It's part of his professional code. I guess he might enjoy the chase.' He shrugged and went to a shelf. 'How's your appetite? I'm getting a little hungry myself.'

Charlie gave a deep unconvincing chuckle. 'You might just as well have invited that Horse Soldier to supper,' he said.

Hawkeye didn't reply. He was too busy looking for something to eat.

★   ★   ★

When the first rays of the sun began to warm the side of the mountain, Sheriff

Wills was still asleep with his wide hat pulled over his eyes. It was a long time since he had slept under the stars like that and he felt his whole frame aching and stiff. He was like a dead man rising in response to the last trump. When he opened his rheumy eyes, he saw a man looking down at him holding a pistol close to his head.

'Feel like getting yourself up?' the man said and Sheriff Wills recognized Horse Soldier.

The sheriff pushed himself up and shivered slightly. The air was too cool to encourage a man to get up even from a hard bed like this.

'So you beat me to it?' he said.

Horse Soldier grinned. His jaw, darkening with stubble, looked like the jaw of the dark angel as the sheriff had seen him in his dreams. Horse Soldier passed over the bottle of whiskey.

Wills declined with a shake of his head. 'Too early in the day. You sleep out here?'

Horse Soldier nodded. 'I sleep

anywhere except in a feather bed. Never could sleep comfortable in a bed.'

Sheriff Wills rolled off his bedroll and shook himself down. The sun was about to reach down into the gully and he was beginning to feel more slightly human. 'I heard the shooting late yesterday,' he said. 'Did you kill Hawkeye Hank?'

Horse Soldier took a swig from his bottle. 'Not yet,' he said. 'I killed three *hombres* gunning for me. Self defence. That's why I'm here. Thought I could use those horses to bring the bodies down to Little Butte, give them proper burial on Boot Hill. A man deserves proper burial even if he is a born killer.'

Sheriff Wills looked him over and decided he was making a strange joke.

'What's your excuse?' Horse Soldier asked him.

'I don't need excuses,' the sheriff said. 'I came up here to prevent a crime. That's my job.'

Horse Soldier chuckled. 'Not up here it isn't. This is way out of your territory.'

Sheriff Wills nodded. He wasn't exactly sure about that. If they took the bodies down to Little Butte it might be his duty to make an arrest and refer the matter to the judge. He started thinking about breakfast. 'What do you aim to do about Hawkeye Hank?' he asked.

Horse Soldier didn't hesitate. He said: 'He'll come back to Texas.'

'Did he agree to that?' the sheriff asked.

'He'll come,' Horse Soldier said. 'It says on the Wanted notice dead or alive. One way or the other he will come.' He spoke as though everything had been arranged according to logic.

Wills opened a can of beans, raked the embers of the fire into life, and started to heat up his breakfast. 'You know, I don't think he will,' he said quietly.

Horse Soldier looked him over and laid his pistol on the ground beside him. 'Maybe you could take those bodies back to Little Butte,' he said. 'Save me a deal of trouble, make things easier.'

Wills stirred his beans and wondered: was this *hombre* cool and determined or was he plain loco? He offered Horse Soldier a mess of beans and started brewing up coffee. Coffee always helped to bring one to life in the morning.

★   ★   ★

Horse Soldier and Wills gathered the bunch of horses together and led them in a string up to Sweet Spring. When Hawkeye Hank saw them coming he opened his mouth slightly and his tongue licked along his upper lip.

'Here they come,' he said to Charlie. 'He's got a whole bunch of horses with him.'

Charlie had rolled off his bed and staggered to the opening. He was holding that Colt revolver in his hand. 'I don't figure this,' he said. 'I think we shoot that Horse Soldier as he comes up here. You shoot him he can't do any more harm.'

'Except there's someone with him and it looks like Sheriff Wills from Little Butte,' Hawkeye said.

Charlie couldn't understand it; he thought he was delirious again. 'What's the sheriff doing here?'

'We'll soon find out,' Hawkeye said.

The bunch of horses and the two riders pulled up short of the hogan and the sheriff dismounted and raised his hand. 'Hi there, Hawkeye,' he greeted. 'We've come to gather up those dead bodies and take them in for burial. Is that OK?'

'OK by me,' Hawkeye replied. He saw that Horse Soldier now had his Winchester held across the saddle. He could swing it across and shoot off a couple of rounds before anyone had a chance to react. 'Don't get fussed, Charlie,' he said quietly. 'Best to play this cool.'

Charlie nodded his big moon face, but he wasn't in the least cool. He had his shooter in his good hand and he was ready to use it. He watched from close

by the entrance to the hogan as Sheriff Wills and Horse Soldier laid the bodies on the backs of the horses and tied them down, arms and legs swinging loose and stiff. There were three bodies. Tod Ridelle still lay spiked somewhere on the rocks below that overhang.

Charlie thought he was in dreamland.

He saw Horse Soldier remount and urge his horse forward towards the hogan. 'Time to go,' Horse Soldier said.

Hawkeye scarcely moved. 'I don't think so,' he said.

Horse Soldier shrugged and held the Winchester on Hawkeye. 'I think it's time,' he said. 'It's down to you, dead or alive, the Wanted notice said. Alive is better. It means you get a fair trial back in Texas. Dead, I still get the reward but you're cold and stiff. Both ways are good but alive is better.'

Hawkeye was smiling but Charlie felt his tension. He gripped his Colt and got ready to use it.

'I think you forgot something,' Hawkeye said.

'I'm sure you're about to remind me.' Horse Soldier raised the Winchester and levelled it at Hawkeye. Charlie looked at Sheriff Wills and thought he was reluctant to intervene. If only I had the use of my good hand, I couldn't miss, he thought.

'You forgot about the gold,' Hawkeye said.

Horse Soldier seemed to relax a little and Charlie saw that he was shaking with silent laughter. 'What gold is that?' he asked.

'The gold I got stashed away for a rainy day,' Hawkeye said. 'The gold I got from that robbery in Texas. You didn't mention that. There could be more gold there than the reward you get from turning me in.'

That seemed to get Horse Soldier thinking. 'So you still got it stashed away somewhere?' he said.

Hawkeye tossed his head. 'What do you think?' he said. 'Maybe that rainy day arrived earlier than expected.'

Horse Soldier was considering his

position. More than the reward dollars, he thought. That's what those stiffs were after: revenge and gold, a potent brew!

'What's the deal?' he said.

Hawkeye shrugged. ' 'We could come to an agreement. I give you the gold and you leave me to live in peace up here to look after my family.'

'That could be so,' Horse Soldier said. 'Where's the stash of gold?'

Hawkeye cocked his head on one side. 'I can't give it to you, not just like that. I can take you to it. That's the deal. You have the gold; I have my family and my life.'

There was a silence. Way off in the mountains they could hear the rumbling of an approaching storm. Charlie was still looking for a way of getting a drop on Horse Soldier. He couldn't believe his friend was acting like a weak kneed jackass. Sheriff Wills was trying to figure things out too; he had no idea which way to jump.

Horse Soldier nodded. 'OK,' he said.

'You get the stash of gold. We have a deal. You go free, I get the gold.'

Hawkeye grinned. 'Not quite so easy as that. I have to find the gold.'

'You mean you got it hidden somewhere?' Horse Soldier said.

Hawkeye was still grinning. He said, 'You don't leave gold hanging around for anyone to steal. A man could creep in while you're sleeping.'

Horse Soldier nodded again. 'I think I savvy. The gold is hidden in those caves behind you.'

'That's the way it is,' Hawkeye agreed.

Horse Soldier was thinking quickly. He wanted that gold but he also wanted Hawkeye. Hawkeye might have reason to slip out through those caves taking the gold with him. Or, if there was no gold, he might escape that way anyway. He could still go after him but it might be a long chase.

'Why don't you send that boy in to bring the gold out?' he suggested.

'Two reasons,' Hawkeye said. 'First is

Manuel doesn't know where the gold is and second he isn't around. We sent him out to find something else. So it's down to me and you. We find it, you get it.'

Horse Soldier paused for a moment. Then he said, 'Why don't we go in there together. You find the gold and the deal is clinched.'

'That's the deal,' Hawkeye agreed.

Horse Soldier dismounted and kept his gun on Hawkeye. 'Put that Colt revolver away,' he said to Charlie. 'It could go off.' He turned to the sheriff. 'Why don't you take those bodies back to Little Butte? That's the best thing you can do.'

Sheriff Wills looked at him and his jaw dropped open in astonishment.

10

On the other side of that buffalo hide curtain it was a lot darker and a lot creepier than Horse Soldier had expected. But he still had his Winchester on Hawkeye Hank and he still had his Colt revolver in its holster. Hawkeye Hank was moving ahead cautiously with a flaming torch held high. The light from it made weird play on the craggy ceiling, but Horse Soldier wasn't superstitious. So he didn't worry unduly on that account.

'You keep two steps ahead of me, you hear?' he said, and his voice echoed out through the cave system like the voices of a hundred dead men.

'I hear you,' Hawkeye said.

'No tricks either,' Horse Soldier warned.

'We don't need tricks here,' Hawkeye's eerie voice replied. 'Don't need to. We got the spirits of the grandfathers.

They don't do tricks either. They just flit around and do what they have to do.' Maybe Hawkeye was joking but Horse Soldier didn't laugh.

'How far in?' he asked.

'Not so far,' Hawkeye echoed back. 'But a man needs to be careful. There's a whole system of twists and turns and different openings here. You go one way and you miss the right turn off.'

'Well, you keep right on.' Horse Soldier motioned with his Winchester. 'We find that stash of gold everything's gonna be OK.'

Hawkeye paused and held the flaming torch up high as though uncertain about which way to go.

'Don't fool with me,' Horse Soldier warned. 'And don't pretend you lost your way.'

Hawkeye Hank looked back over his shoulder but Horse Soldier betrayed no fear. Maybe he hadn't enough imagination to be afraid. 'I'm looking for something,' Hawkeye said.

'I thought you knew where the gold

was?' Horse Soldier said. He brought the Winchester up to his shoulder and held it level. 'Don't fool around. You know where that gold is, you find it. That was the deal.'

'Then we find our way out again,' Hawkeye chuckled.

Then Horse Soldier knew the half Navajo, half gringo, might be intent on leading him astray. 'You take me there and take me out again,' he said. 'Otherwise one of us is liable to come out dead.'

Hawkeye didn't reply to that. He was listening. He knew by instinct and experience that, apart from the echo of their voices, there was something else. This was a high part of the cave and he held up his torch to see the roof which seemed to soar more than a mile above.

'Cave opens out here,' he said. There were crags and even projections above where a man might walk upright. He raised the flaming torch. 'We have to climb up there if we want the gold.'

Horse Soldier saw that it was quite a

climb. He thought of sending Hawkeye on alone but that was no good. It would give Hawkeye the advantage. Hawkeye knew the way and he had the torch. 'OK, we climb,' he said. 'You go first and remember I've got the gun on you. You make a false move and you're dead meat.'

Hawkeye Hank chuckled and his voice seemed to stretch out for ever down the echoing cave. 'Dead meat isn't gonna lead you to that pot of gold,' he declared. 'Only living, breathing flesh can do that.'

Horse Soldier gestured impatiently with his Winchester. 'You just lead on,' he said.

Hawkeye was about to put his foot on the first part of the climb when he turned. 'You take care now,' he said. 'These rocks can be goddamned slippery. A man could injure himself to death climbing up here.'

Horse Soldier gestured with the gun again. 'Just climb,' he said. 'I'll take care of the slippery.'

Hawkeye turned to face the rock. He reached with his left hand for a secure hold, but before he could lever himself up a dark form flew towards him and veered off to the right. There was a series of high pitched squeaks as a host of ghostly forms darted down the gloomy passage directly towards them. Even Horse Soldier ducked instinctively to avoid them.

'You don't need to worry about bats,' he heard Hawkeye Hank say. 'They just live in this part of the cave. It's their territory.' He laughed, looking back at Horse Soldier. He saw that Horse Soldier wasn't spooked. It took a hell of a lot to spook this crazy bounty hunter. Hawkeye began the ascent. He took one step up the steep and slippery slope and stopped. There was a sound from above and it wasn't bats or bears. It sounded like the slithering movement a human body might make.

'You hear that noise?' he said.

'I hear it,' Horse Soldier replied laconically.

'Like I mentioned,' Hawkeye said. 'This a place for the grandfathers. You don't see them but you feel them and they see you.'

Horse Soldier made a low growling noise of dissent. Was this Hawkeye trying to wind him up?

Then came a cry. It was shrill and high and it set up a serious of echoes that ran right through the shivering caves and froze the marrow of a man's bones.

Horse Soldier stood as still as a carved figurehead. Then he raised the Winchester as though searching for a target. The next instant a rock came bouncing down and hit him right on the shoulder. He drew back and fired a deafening shot towards where he figured the rock had come from.

Hawkeye was ready. He took his cue and he swung round and flung the flaming torch at Horse Soldier's face. It hit Horse Soldier close to his head and snatched his black Stetson away, flaming and bowling into the darkness

like some kind of Catherine wheel.

Horse Soldier was fond of that hat. It was part of his character and he felt naked without it. So he cursed and flung out at Hawkeye ... just a moment too late. Hawkeye got a grip on the hot Winchester, twisted it, and attempted to wrench it from Horse Soldier's grasp. For several seconds the two men wrestled over the Winchester and then there was another deafening explosion and Horse Soldier staggered but kept his hold on the gun. The Winchester was useless anyway. He could never swing it and lever it for a third shot before Hawkeye wrenched it away. The barrel was burning hot anyway. So Horse Soldier twisted again and the Winchester came out of Hawkeye's grasp. Horse Soldier beat down with the Winchester on Hawkeye's shoulder and Hawkeye staggered away. Horse Soldier hurled the Winchester down and reached for his Colt. He had it half drawn when Hawkeye came in head down to butt the wind

out of his chest.

Horse Soldier staggered back with the Colt half drawn, but before he could yank it free and fire a shot, the whole cave seemed to flicker and blank out. Something or someone, human or ghostly, had extinguished the torch. The Stetson had bowled away round the passage to be swallowed in the black interior.

Horse Soldier thumbed back the hammer and fired at Hawkeye, or where he figured Hawkeye would be. But Hawkeye could move fast too and the crash of the shot seemed to echo down the halls of eternity.

'You think you double crossed me!' Horse Soldier snarled and fired another shot.

'You double crossed yourself,' Hawkeye echoed back from close to his ear.

Horse Soldier fired again and a shower of splintered rock spurted from the side of the cave.

'You gotta practise your aim better,' Hawkeye mocked. 'Or why don't you

throw away that useless shooter and fight like a real man?'

Horse Soldier beat the air with his revolver hoping to pistol whip Hawkeye but without making contact. He fired another round and thought he saw in the flash the dim shadow of a human form. He cocked the Colt and fired again.

'That's five rounds,' Hawkeye said, from a different direction close by. 'Why don't you blast off that last round and reload. You could be luckier next time.'

That's what you'd like, Horse Soldier thought. But I have other thoughts. He held the Colt high and made himself steady and still to listen. He could hear Hawkeye's breathing quite close by and to his left another sound, low, like an animal slithering towards him. Could it be one of those spooks Hawkeye had talked about? Keep yourself still, he thought. Keep yourself as still as a rock and just listen.

Everything became quiet as the grave

as though troops of dead men were listening and waiting. He couldn't even locate Hawkeye's breathing and the slithering noise had stopped . . . but those spooks were not far out of reach!

Then someone seemed to turn up the lights. The flames in Horse Soldier's Stetson had taken hold and the whole cave shone with a dim flickering radiance. Horse Soldier stood poised with his Colt revolver and he saw Hawkeye crouching no more than six feet away. The Winchester lay on the floor of the cave between them. From the corner of his eye to the left he saw another figure also poised like a cat, ready to strike. Like a big cat or maybe the ghost of a dead Navajo brave, or maybe even a projecting rock. Horse couldn't be sure.

He brought his Colt down to cover Hawkeye. 'This one's for you,' he said. 'That Wanted notice said dead or alive. It's your choice.'

Hawkeye Hank made no move. Maybe he was an illusion too. Down

there in that dim cave everything seemed possible.

'It's your choice,' Horse Soldier repeated.

Now he could see the rise and fall of Hawkeye's breathing and knew he was a creature from the living world.

Then Hawkeye spoke and his voice cut though the darkness like the edge of a flint arrow. 'You know something,' he said. 'You are one damned fool. I thought you were living in the world of the sane but now I know you're just full of pride and horse shit and just as greedy as any other living man.'

'If that's what you think, think again,' Horse Soldier said. He drew back the hammer of his Colt and held it waist high to cover any movement Hawkeye might make. He saw Hawkeye glance down at the Winchester and knew he was getting ready to make a dive for it.

From the corner of his eye he saw something else too. The crouching ghost had moved. As his eye was diverted towards it, it came like a

railroad train straight for his lower legs.

That momentary deflection was enough for Hawkeye and he moved with the speed of light. He was on Horse Soldier in an instant. Horse Soldier didn't know what had hit him. His legs buckled. His Colt was hurled to one side and a fist slammed into his teeth. His head jerked back against the rocky side of the cave and he slid down slowly to the floor of the cave.

The boy Manuel seized the Colt revolver and levelled it at Horse Soldier's head. 'I kill him! I kill him!' he shouted in a frenzy . . . and he meant it.

'No,' Hawkeye said. 'There's enough blood spilled. Give me the gun!'

Manuel hesitated a moment and then relinquished the revolver. Hawkeye thrust it through his belt. He bent down and turned Horse Soldier over onto his face. Then he took out a length of rawhide he had in his pouch and tied the man's hands behind his back. Then he stooped and raised Horse Soldier up on the wall of the cave.

Horse Soldier's eyes flickered open and he shook his head. 'You didn't kill me,' he muttered.

Hawkeye Hank got hold of him by the collar and yanked him clear of the wall. 'Didn't need to,' he said. 'You might just as well have killed yourself.'

The boy Manuel retrieved what was left of the flaming Stetson and rekindled the torch from it.

'Now we get ourselves out of here,' Hawkeye Hank said.

Horse Soldier shook his head clear and said: 'You got a brave kid here.'

'Don't call me a kid. I'm a man,' Manuel boasted.

'I think you could be right about that,' Horse Soldier agreed.

Hawkeye Hank gave him a shove and they made their way back through the labyrinth towards the hogan.

★ ★ ★

Charlie was pacing up and down with his gun in his hand. He had heard the

sound of shots from the labyrinth and he feared the worst.

'I should have been in there,' he raved.

'Now you just keep yourself calm and quiet,' Sheriff Wills said. 'You lost too much blood already. You're in no fit state to creep about in a cave looking for more trouble.' He knew that if anyone had gone into that cave it should have been him. But he was getting too old to crawl about in caves. Like his wife said, it was time for him to retire. He had heard the shots echoing through the caves and he too feared the worst. It sounded like a whole regiment had been feuding in there and he didn't see how any man could have survived.

Then he heard voices coming from the deep interior, and, drawing back the buffalo curtain, he saw the flickering light and the figures approaching. Next moment they took shape in the darkness. The two men were smeared and streaked with blood and the boy looked like a rooster crowing on a hill.

Horse Soldier stepped out into the light and shook his head. He still had that hard defiant look in his eyes but, without his black Stetson, he looked somewhat diminished.

'Set yourself down over there.' Hawkeye prodded Horse Soldier with his own Winchester. That was when Wills noticed that Horse Soldier's hands were tied behind his back. 'So you didn't get yourself killed after all,' he said to Hawkeye.

'That was never my intention,' Hawkeye said with a chuckle. 'I got too many responsibilities around here.'

Wills nodded. 'What do you aim to do with this bounty hunter?' he asked.

Horse Soldier raised his head with a wry grin. 'Before you decide on that,' he said. 'I have one request. There's a small bottle of whiskey standing out there some place. You give me a drink of that stuff, I'll be ready.'

Hawkeye and Charlie looked at Manuel and Charlie cocked his head on one side. Manuel went out to search for

the bottle of whiskey. When he got to the entrance, he turned. 'Didn't tell you something, did I?' he said.

All eyes turned to look at him.

'What was that?' Hawkeye said.

'What was that?' Charlie asked a fraction of a second later.

Manuel came back into the room. 'It's Meralito. I forgot to tell you Meralito's had her baby right there as I watched.'

Hawkeye opened his mouth in astonishment. 'You mean she just had her baby?'

Manuel looked slightly abashed as though he shouldn't have been there watching the proceedings. 'It happened a while back. Nino helped her. They're right there at the other end of the cave. Meralito's resting. And the baby was howling real good when I left.'

'Why didn't you tell us this before?' Charlie had a huge grin on his face.

'Didn't have too much time,' Manuel said wryly. 'Had work to do with Hawkeye, didn't I?'

'Is it a girl or a boy?' Hawkeye gasped.

'I think it's a girl,' Manuel said. 'I didn't ask.'

Hawkeye leaned forward. 'You mean Meralito is out there in the open with the baby?'

'The baby's OK,' Manuel protested. 'Nino is looking out for everything. She covered Meralito with a blanket.'

'We got to get them in here.' Hawkeye Hank moved to the back of the hogan and turned. 'I've got to get them in here,' he said again.

And he disappeared.

★ ★ ★

'I've never seen a man move so quick,' Sheriff Wills said to his wife two days later. 'That Hawkeye was as proud a father as any man I've met. He just disappeared before we could hardly look at him. But you know,' he shrugged, 'those Navajo women are as tough as rawhide. Sure, Meralito had

had that papoose out there in the open and no harm came to either of them. Nino knew exactly what to do. They had wanted to get up to the Chelly Canyon but there was no way they could do that before the baby was born. It was more than a day's ride, maybe more. So they just hunkered down and she had that baby right out in the open like they do. And it was a girl too.'

Maria Wills gave him a withering look. 'You wouldn't know about Navajo women or any other women. No man would,' she said.

Wills nodded. 'Maybe so, maybe so.' He wasn't into arguing with his wife.

'So that left you to bring in those dead men?' she said.

The sheriff shrugged. 'Had to. Least I could do. You don't just dump four dead corpses and leave them to the coyotes and the buzzards. That wouldn't be decent like, would it?'

Maria gave him a hard look but she had to agree. 'Then why aren't they here?' she asked.

The whole episode had been weird, Sheriff Wills conceded. The sheriff of Little Butte riding down the mountain with four dead bodies and a bounty hunter with no bounty and his hands tied with rawhide in front of him across his saddle. Though Wills didn't have a particularly rich imagination he could see the funny side.

'What do you aim to do?' Horse Soldier asked. 'These dead men are starting to stink real bad.'

Sheriff Wills didn't need to be reminded of that. His sense of smell was as good as any man's. 'You got a suggestion?' he said.

'Sure do.' Horse Soldier raised his head. 'When we get lower down among the foothills the ground will be a deal softer. Why don't we just dig a pit and lay these dead men in it with their hands crossed on the chests nice and peaceful like a bunch of saints?'

Wills regarded him in some astonishment. 'As I recall, these *hombres* tried to kill you.'

Horse Soldier nodded. 'They did their best,' he said. 'A man does his best he deserves a proper burial.' He looked up and grinned. 'Specially if he is beginning to stink like that.'

Wills couldn't deny the last part. 'But we don't have anything to dig with, do we?'

Horse Soldier nodded and grinned again. 'We do that,' he said. 'I have a trenching tool here by my side. Always carry it. Comes in useful from time to time.'

Wills considered the matter. 'That would be a lot of digging,' he said.

'Half as much if we do it together,' Horse Soldier said. 'It doesn't need to be too deep. Just enough to cover them. Then we pile rocks on top. Even mark the place with a cross if we had a mind to it.'

Wills thought about it. The man's a killer, he figured. He has something

tricky up his sleeve. 'I don't think we can do that,' he said. He thought about riding into Little Butte with the four stinking bodies and Horse Soldier. But that posed problems. What would he do with Horse Soldier anyway?

'Yes, we can do that,' Horse Soldier insisted. 'We take it turn and turn about. Or I can dig and you can watch. Or maybe you could roll up rocks and pile them on top. They call it working together.'

That was a weird picture too. Wills would need to cut Horse Soldier's bonds and trust him. Horse Soldier was a dangerous *hombre*. But then again, what would happen when they reached Little Butte? Would he put Horse Soldier in the hoosegow and wait on the judge? On what charge? the judge might ask him. What would be the answer? This man is a bounty hunter and he nearly got himself killed doing his profession. The judge might find that difficult to find in the book rules.

Horse Soldier seemed to read his

thoughts. 'You're well outside your territory here, Sheriff,' he said. 'What happened in Sweet Spring was none of your concern. Self-defence anyway. You could say I killed those killers to stop them killing Hawkeye Hank. How does that figure with you?'

Wills shook his head. 'It doesn't figure with me at all. You wanted Hawkeye dead yourself for that reward.' He pondered on the matter. 'I loose your bonds, you do the digging while I watch. Then we discuss the matter a little more.'

Horse Soldier gave him a shrewd look as though he was weighing things up. 'OK, you got a deal here,' he said. 'I have no argument with you anyway.'

When they reached the lower lands, they drew rein. Horse Soldier produced his digging tool, chose a likely spot, and started to dig. He was good and strong even after the ruckus in the cave and, after quite a short time, they had a shallow grave into which they laid the corpses as Horse Soldier had suggested.

Each body lay face up with its hands crossed on its chest and its hat covering its face.

'Look kind of saintly, don't they?' Horse Soldier remarked.

Sheriff Wills was astonished and impressed. He thought Horse Soldier might even mutter a prayer or two.

'Now we pile rocks on top,' Horse Soldier said.

Together they built up quite a megalith of rocks.

Horse Soldier mounted up. 'You know what,' he said thoughtfully. 'I should have used my brains. I don't believe there ever was any gold in those caves and I was a fool to believe there was.' He settled himself comfortably in the saddle and looked across at Wills.

'I don't believe there was,' Wills conceded. 'If there ever had been Hawkeye Hank must have given it away to those Navajo. Make up a little for what Kit Carson did in the Chelly Canyon way back.'

Horse Soldier shrugged. 'I was a

damned fool to think otherwise.' He sat for a moment pondering. 'Tell you something, anyway. I didn't come into this wild country for the bounty. I came for the challenge and I lost out to that Hawkeye who can't make up his mind whether he's a white man or an Indian.' He paused again to reflect. 'Good with his fists though.' He turned his horse and looked back over his shoulder. 'Pity about that Jude Riverwind too. He was just eaten up with envy and jealousy for Hawkeye Hank and his woman. So maybe we did them a favour. Those Navajo rugs the woman makes are something else again. I could take one myself, 'cept I don't have anywhere to take it.' He grinned and nodded at the sheriff. '*Adios amigo*,' he said mockingly, and the sheriff watched him as he rode away.

★ ★ ★

'What about Jude Riverwind?' Maria Wills asked. 'What happened to him?'

'I can't answer that,' the sheriff said whimsically. 'That Manuel boy said he killed him with a stone but I'm not sure about it. Could be he's still wandering about up there dazed as a broken horse close by the Sweet Spring but that's Hawkeye Hank's problem, not mine.'

'And Horse Soldier?' she asked. 'You think he rode back to Texas.'

'Guess so,' Sheriff Wills said. He sucked on his empty pipe for a while. Never can tell with a man like that. But one thing's for certain. He won't bother Hawkeye Hank any more. When he saw how Hawkeye cares for his family, I think he figured to let the whole thing drop. That's his code — his sense of honour.'

'You could have claimed that reward yourself,' Maria Wills said.

The sheriff laughed loud and clear. 'You know what,' he said. 'You're right about one thing: it's time for me to hang up my spurs and retire.'

We do hope that you have enjoyed reading this large print book.

Did you know that all of our titles are available for purchase?

We publish a wide range of high quality large print books including:
Romances, Mysteries, Classics
General Fiction
Non Fiction and Westerns

Special interest titles available in large print are:
The Little Oxford Dictionary
Music Book, Song Book
Hymn Book, Service Book

Also available from us courtesy of Oxford University Press:
Young Readers' Dictionary
(large print edition)
Young Readers' Thesaurus
(large print edition)

For further information or a free brochure, please contact us at:
Ulverscroft Large Print Books Ltd.,
The Green, Bradgate Road, Anstey,
Leicester, LE7 7FU, England.
Tel: (00 44) **0116 236 4325**
Fax: (00 44) **0116 234 0205**

Other titles in the
Linford Western Library:

CALEB BLOOD

P. McCormac

Caleb Blood was a man who'd seen too much bloodletting. He tried to forget, but despite the whiskey, his demons — past and present — wouldn't let him alone. All the things he should cherish were being stripped from his life. There was no option but to take up arms again. Once the guns were unlimbered, the death toll mounted and he faced so many enemies it seemed he had no chance of survival. When, he wondered, would the killing end?